PRAY FOR JUSTICE

ON THE TRAIL WITH ORRIN PORTER ROCKWELL

Marc Otte

**Two Modern-day Marshals Face
the Challenge of Their Lives with
Help from Beyond the Veil**

PUBLICATION
CONSULTANTS
We Believe In The Power Of Authors

PO Box 221974 Anchorage, Alaska 99522-1974

ISBN 1-888125-19-5

Library of Congress Catalog Card Number: 97-69007

Cover painting by Richard Pope
Other art by Marc Otte

Manufactured in the United States of America.

FOR VICTORIA

ACKNOWLEDGMENTS

I gratefully thank the folks who helped turn this idea into a story in one way or another: first, Steve and Theresa Thompson for reading the fledgling manuscript and giving editorial comment; also, Denny, John, Rob, Jerry, Lannie, Roger, Marc G., Horace, Monte, Gladys, Cody, Shawn, and George—heroes all—any of which I'd go through the darkest door with and gladly call my partner; and most especially—Ty Cunningham; my sensei, my comrade at arms—and my friend.

CHAPTER 1
Saturday

To a dog, horse toenails are pure ambrosia and Belle was no exception. The squat, broad faced Queensland heeler lay on her belly in the dry pine needles and chewed on a curling crescent of fresh hoof. She kept a soft, brown eye on her man; partly because she felt it her job to take care of him and partly because she knew more chunks of smelly hoof would be coming her way.

Skip Garret stood hunched over like an upside down human V, toes pointed in, the back leg of a stout, roman-nosed bay across his left thigh. Low rays of morning sun filtered through a dense stand of Douglas fir along the driveway and cast a long, orange shadow over the dusty ground. The September air was cool enough for the big man to see his breath, but warm enough that horseshoing made wearing a jacket unnecessary.

Dressed in a faded denim shirt with his jeans tucked into the stovepipe shafts of black bull hide boots, Garret looked like a man from a different time. He dressed not so much for looks as utility. The calfskin stampede string hanging down behind his head was there to keep his hat from falling off at a gallop, and the canary yellow scarf kept his neck warm and doubled as a hand towel or dust mask. He would never admit, not even to himself, that he wanted to emulate any sort of style. Everything was practical and had a practical use. It just seemed that lately the world had developed a liking for his sort of dress and he happened to be in vogue.

Skip had been up since before dawn, having woken in a melancholy mood, the thought of Brenda throbbing in his mind like a bad tooth. It had been almost a year since she quit him. Sometimes at night he still dreamed about her and woke up feeling heartsick. Not so much because he wanted her to come back; Brenda Jo had been a difficult woman to live with. He usually just woke up angry with himself for being so dim headed about the whole relationship. He supposed she considered him a moron for not realizing early something was wrong with their marriage. She accused him of spending more time chasing bandits than he spent chasing her, but he had assumed a woman who would wait two years for a missionary would wait just as patiently for him to catch an outlaw or two. He was wrong.

Of course the Bishop had counseled, "Try and work it out. Two righteous people ought to be capable of a happy marriage."

Later though, the Bishop took Skip aside in the wide, dim hallway of the chapel. "I don't know how to tell you this, son ... but she's given up." A surgeon in secular life, the man spoke with cutting precision. As Bishop, he was indeed blessed with a discerning spirit. Not long after the hallway talk, Brenda moved out and he was served with papers.

Once awake, Garret chased the thoughts of ex-wives from his brain. The endless list of Saturday chores demanded his attention. Between work and church he was forced to cram as much into each Saturday as he could, just to keep up with his place.

You'd think he never fed the buttermilk-dun mare the way she ate the corral wood. Several of the top rails by the water trough needed to be replaced. He had reshod her and the pack mule the week before but put off re-shoeing Jake.

Horseshoeing can be brutally hard on a back if a person is particularly tall. Especially when it isn't done on a regular basis. Skip stood a hair over six feet two and even on a tall horse, like Jake, he had to do a lot of bending over to get down close to the work.

Having been taught to shoe as a youngster on a ranch near Ft. Worth, he considered making it a career for a time. The money was good and it paid for college and a mission to Japan. His father had been right though, when he pointed out that a man as big as Skip who couldn't make a living with his head higher than his rear-end wasn't a very smart man. Now he just did his own stock and saved a couple of hundred bucks every month or two in the process.

The smoke colored heeler sat on her haunches, close enough to sniff the bottom of Jake's hoof, her small head cocked to one side. She stared intently at Skip's work with the nippers and licked her lips in anticipation. Having already pulled the old shoe, Skip pared away the flaky sole with the curved blade of a hoof knife, making himself a grooved guide. Droplets of sweat formed along his brow despite the cool morning air.

Making certain to keep the nippers level and working from one side of the heel to the other, he snipped off a crescent of overgrown hoof about a quarter of an inch thick and tossed it to the heeler. Her broad dark lips pulled back showing perfect white fangs when she grasped the smelly morsel of toenail. Smiling a contented smile, she flopped down on the spot to enjoy her treat. Still bent over almost double, Skip scratched the black patch of fur on her head. She stuck her nose up to meet him and groaned. Easy to please, the dog greeted each piece of hoof trimming like her first prize of the day.

Using the slender nipper handles, Skip snagged the blunt end of a wide shoeing rasp on the ground by his boot and flicked it up to his other hand. The fewer times he had to bend all the way to the ground, the better his back would feel later. The big gelding, used to the routine, kept his leg relaxed … until the buzzing started. No horse not even one as well trained as Jake is fond of a bumblebee. Since horses know nothing of vibrating pagers, when Skip's began to buzz under its outstretched leg, visions of bumblebee exploded into its tiny horse brain; big, mean, horse eating bumblebees.

Skip felt the gelding's muscles tighten at the same time he realized his pager was going off. By then it was too late. The stout bay drew his leg forward with such force it threw Skip backward, lifting him off his feet and planting him on the dusty ground ten feet away. The combination of a horse leg capable of moving a thousand pound animal, and the jolting impact of the hard packed ground, knocked the wind out of him. Fortunately though, he landed on his more padded parts and would probably end up with nothing more than a nasty, wallet shaped bruise. Jake rattled an angry snort and pawed the earth with a large forefoot. His eyes rolled back, whites showing, and his ears pinned in annoyance.

The blue heeler wisely retreated to safety behind a thick red fir tree. This horse had more than once sent her sprawling and she knew from personal experience how hard it could kick. Still holding the piece of hoof trimming between her teeth, the heeler trotted over and sniffed her man's boot. He scratched her behind the ears and hauled himself to his feet with a long, slow groan. Once she saw he was alright, she settled down again to her chewing.

Skip dusted himself off and calmed his jigging horse. "It's just a page Jakie boy. It's bound to hurt me a lot more than it'll hurt you."

At the sound of Skip's deep, soothing voice the bay relaxed at once with a deep, growling sigh. Skip glanced at the horse eating pager on his belt. The little black plastic box that had more than once played wrecking ball with his weekend and wondered vaguely what Wyatt Earp or Porter Rockwell would have done with such a thing. Probably toss it in the air and blast it to smithereens. He grinned an evil grin at the prospect. As he had suspected, it was the office. Hardly a weekend went by that they didn't page for some reason or another.

Skip turned the gelding out in his paddock and slid the horseshoe gate latch shut. "Sorry Jake, I have to go in for a minute. I've still got two feet to do, so I guess you'll have to walk around lop sided for a bit."

Jake turned away and trotted over to the metal hay bunk pinning his ears to shoo away a stocky dun mare. A muscular red mule with a torn ear trotted away after her. Lopsided or not, Mr. Jake was still in charge.

Skip took one long, deep whiff of the paddock smell before heading toward the house. Brenda thought it asinine, but he loved the smell of horse sweat, hay, and manure. Being around them was one of his greatest pleasures.

Taking off his battered grey felt hat, Skip walked inside. He lived alone and could have worn a hat in the house all he wanted, but deep in his heart he felt the ghost of his dead father would swoop out of nowhere and knock it off his head.

His house was small but neat. He lived simply and didn't need a large place after Brenda gave him the boot. She moved back to Dallas and he rented a trailer here. Hard hearted as she turned out to be, Brenda was no money grubber and when the divorce was final, Skip found he could afford a small place in the country.

Skip did most of his living at the office and had really bought this place for the spacious, four stall barn and sprawling corrals. Still, his tastes were adequate, and the two bedroom log home had been well decorated. His sister Marie had a strong taste for things Southwest, and it showed in the furniture she helped him pick out. The rich rust of the Indian blanket patterns on the furniture complemented the two antique saddles on wooden racks at either end of the couch. A pair of Henry rifles, he inherited from his father, hung on the mantle above a river-stone fireplace.

Apart from the couch and matching easy chair, the furnishings were sparse. He was hardly ever home and when he was, he stayed outside, so the place remained as clean as a western heritage museum. Skip had a seat with his name on it at the cafe up the road. When he did take a meal at home, he ate at the small, knotty pine bar in the kitchen, where the phone was.

He tossed his hat on one of the two wooden barstools and sat on the other, being careful not to scratch the light wood with his spurs. Picking up the phone with one hand, he punched the speed dial to the office. With his free hand he took a comb from his shirt pocket and absent mindedly combed through the chocolate handlebar mustache obscuring his upper lip. The length of time it took for the office to answer was usually in direct proportion to the urgency of the page. The line rang twice; maybe this wasn't going to be much after all. Skip's back was tired from shoeing Jake, and he didn't mind the rest.

A woman's voice answered the phone in the middle of the third ring. "Marshals office." The answer was short and matter of fact. The kind of voice you hear on an answering machine. A government voice.

Skip stopped combing his mustache. "Yeah Sherry, it's Garret. Did you page me?"

There was a pause, and Skip thought he heard a sob or maybe just a cough. "Sorry to bother you on a weekend Skip." The voice had actually taken on a personality now. Sherry Prather was a new clerk, only aboard a year. She was eager and a good trooper. "Hang on a minute. Terry's here. He wants to talk to you."

"Terry? I thought he was going fishing this morning with his boys."

"Just hang on okay?" There was that sob again. This time it was definitely a sob.

Skip found himself on hold before Terry McGreggor came on the line. Partners for the last three years, Terry and he had become fast friends as soon as Skip transferred to Montana. His wife Christina had also taken an instant liking to Skip and helped out emotionally when Brenda was calling it quits with the marriage. The two were like brothers: seldom apart for long, even when not at work.

"Skipper?" Terry's soft, raspy voice came on the line. It was solemn and deliberate.

"What's up Terry?" Skip was beginning to get a pit in his stomach. He could read his partners mood over the phone.

"I've got hard news …" Terry's voice trailed off then he coughed. "Wally Fuller was killed this morning." The line fell silent again.

Wally was a Montana Highway Patrolman and a mutual friend. The three men each bagged elk the previous fall in the Bitterroot. Besides police work, Wally attended the same ward and shared the gospel in common with his two friends. Mormon policemen weren't exactly unheard of in Montana but they weren't the norm either. The men soon found they had much more than just work or the gospel in common and shared a camaraderie few members of the elders quorum could even imagine.

"Killed?" Skip breathed out hard. Concentrating his thoughts, he ran a hand through his sweaty hair. "What happened?" His voice sounded weak, even to himself.

"Three outlaws escaped from Deer Lodge Prison last night. They're bad ones Skip. Wally must have spotted something around four this morning at the rest area east of town on I 90. Who knows, maybe he was just stretching his legs."

"He never checked out with dispatch?" Skip asked.

"No. A truck driver from Spokane found him at four thirty this morning ... Skip, they beat him to death with a piece of sprinkler pipe." Terry Mcgreggor, who rarely showed any emotion even in the middle of a brawl, was hardly talking above a whisper.

"They must have taken him from behind." Skip said, bitter gall climbing up his throat. "Wally was too big a man to let someone get to him with a pipe without one heck of a fight."

"That's what I figure. Anyway, there's more. They took his pistol, the Mini 14 and a shotgun from his car. The state boys don't carry as much extra ammo as you and I do, but they figure Wally had a couple of extra mags for the mini and maybe two or three boxes of buckshot for the twelve gauge. With what they took from his pistol belt, that makes them pretty well armed."

Skip shook his head and rubbed a calloused hand across his face in disbelief. "Have we got files on the bandits?" All this talk of a dead friend made him very tired.

"Sherry's working on that. The prison is faxing some stuff to us now. No one has officially asked for our help, but they don't mind having us around. Why don't you come in and we can form a game plan." Terry's voice was less somber when he talked about getting to work. It was something to focus on at least. "State investigators are staging a meeting at ten thirty. If you hurry we'll have a chance to talk before they start."

"I won't even change clothes." Skip started to hang up but a sudden thought made his stomach ache. "What about Tracy? Has anyone told her?"

"Christina is with her now. I think the Bishop is on his way over there too."

"Does she know what happened?"

"Partially," Terry said. "The Highway Patrol sent some people over to break the news. Christina took the boys to our house. They know something's up, but they don't know what ... yet."

Skip felt the bitterness in his throat again and for a moment, thought he might throw up. He had a strong stomach when it came to most things, but once in a while it rebelled.

The thought of the Fuller's ten and four-year old boys without a father brought on waves of anger and nausea. He took a deep breath and drummed his fingers on the pale wood of the counter. Luckily, he was able to do something about the people responsible. That would make him feel less helpless.

"I'll be there in twenty minutes," he said and hung up the phone.

Splashing cold water from the kitchen faucet on his face to clear his head, Skip paused only long enough to strap on his forty five, then headed for Missoula.

Belle, the smoke colored heeler chewed on her horse hoof and watched him disappear down the road in his white Ford Bronco. He left often …, but he always came back.

CHAPTER 2

The mountains northwest of Alberton, Montana are not bad if you have a map and are in reasonably decent shape. The trouble was, Pete didn't know exactly where they were, and he was the only one of the three who wasn't carrying around at least twenty extra pounds. In addition to being overweight, the kid had the added problem of his jaw. That big trooper knocked it out of place along with two top teeth when they first jumped him. Pete had known enough to stay clear, but the boy had been much too eager. The jaw wasn't fractured, just dislocated, but the pain was so bad, Pete had to set it back in place before the kid would move from the rest area. He had babbled and screamed so loud, Pete decided he would have to shoot him. In the end though, resetting the jaw quieted him down sufficiently.

Now his flabby, pockmarked face was badly swollen and his left eye was glazed over with a film of dried red blood. His mood had always been sullen when he was in prison, but now it was vile, and he stumbled along behind the others carrying the shotgun and threatening to shoot to death the next person they came across. Beads of sweat formed on his forehead and upper lip, matting dirty blond hair to his pallid skin. They had to keep to the woods to avoid detection from the air and the elk trail they followed was steep and rocky. Every step he took shot spasms of pain through the left side of his head. Because of the missing teeth, even breathing was painful.

"I don't understand why we couldn't just keep his car." the kid whined.

Pete shook his head violently. He had been over all this once already when they stashed the dead cop's patrol car. The rickety old barn looked

14

abandoned. It would take days for anyone to find it if they ever did. "We might as well give ourselves up if we did that." Miller leaned his hand against the rough, rusty bark of a fir tree and took a deep breath. It was difficult to talk to people as stupid as these two. "The highways are the first place the cops will look. We have to stick to the plan. They won't figure anyone would be stupid enough to try and make it over these mountains without any food or shelter."

"They may have a point," moaned the man between Pete and the kid. "I have got to sit."

Carl Meeks was the tallest of the group at six feet four. Even three years of prison life had not gotten rid of his ponderous beer belly and he was sweating almost as badly as the younger man. He had been a football player in high school and a good one at that. But shortly after graduation, he became nothing more than a football watcher, and the closest thing to exercise he participated in was beating his wife. She left him early on, and then he didn't even get that for a workout. The big-bellied man sat on a long cedar blow-down. Leaning the Mini 14 rifle against a stump, he rubbed his left knee.

The little puke hero of a clerk at the last store he robbed had hit a silent alarm, and the cops had shot him in the leg and shoulder. That was the thing with cops, if they killed you it was a fluke. Most of them just weren't killers; they were family men and didn't make their bullets count. He figured the shot actually saved his life in the long run. If he hadn't been wounded, he probably would have killed the young police-man and ended up in the electric chair.

Pete turned and looked in disgust at the two other men, shaking his head. "Okay, we'll rest here for a few minutes. We need to find a place to get some warmer clothes. Jimmy, how far is it to that cabin you were talking about?"

"It's Jim," said the young man with the swollen face, his voice muffled by his oversized jaw. He collapsed on the ground beside the log and leaned his throbbing head against it. "I told you, I don't want to be called Jimmy."

Pete eyed him thoughtfully. He could have put a bullet in his head right then, but that wouldn't have been prudent. He still needed him to get out of Montana. There was, after all, strength in numbers. As long as the kid didn't get too insolent, Pete needed him alive. "Whatever you say, Jim. Do you even know where we are?"

"Yeah, we're out of that stinkin' hole we've been in." He sat up and gingerly rubbed his bloody eye. He looked up at the old man, ahead of him on the trail. He was dangerous, that was certain. There was always a thinly veiled threat in his tone and it was best not to push him too far. "We're probably about a day away."

"You sure you know this country, Jim?" the pot bellied man on the log said. The trees and under brush were thick and his leg was hurting from all this back woods stuff. He needed to find the cabin soon. There were supposed to be horses there and although he had never been on a horse before in his life, it had to be better than walking.

Jim gave the fat man a cold stare. "I know where we are Carl, okay."

"I hope so, because that's why we brought you." said Carl.

"Shut up both of you," demanded Pete, seeing where this was headed. Paunchy, stupid Carl was right, but he saw no reason to get into it with the boy now, not yet. Beyond that, Pete didn't want the youngster pointing out to Carl why he was needed on the trip. Carl had been to Canada before and knew people there. In fact the idea of escaping had been his. He was just a dreamer and a talker though, and didn't have near enough sense to pull it off by himself. He was just dumb enough to think Pete brought him along because they were cell mates.

Pete pitched one of the dead trooper's canteens to Carl. "You two take a drink and then lets get going. Jim says we're a day away, so we're a day away." With that, he turned and surveyed the trail ahead of them.

Jim spat a mouth full of trail dust on the needle covered forest floor. "How long do you think it will be before they come after us?" He said, more out of curiosity than fear.

"Oh," said Pete without turning around. "They're after us now. They just don't know where to start." He looked above him. The thick canopy of trees protected them from air searches and tracking through these mountains would be like looking for the proverbial needle. "This country is big enough to hide us I think … if you boys will get to your feet sometime today."

Pete glanced at the watch, a Seiko Diver. A big one, with a stainless steel band and a luminous face and it still had blood on the crystal. He unfastened the band and rubbed the watch face against his grubby jeans. The blood in no way repulsed him. It didn't matter that it belonged to the man he killed earlier in the day. It just made it hard to tell the time. Holding the watch up in the twilight atmosphere of the forest, he looked it over. Water resistant to one hundred meters, was printed on the back. Just below that, in letters barely large enough to read, a jeweler had etched "I love you, Tracy."

Must have been his wife, Pete thought as he strapped the timepiece back on his left wrist. He looked at its face again. Much better. The time was eleven ten AM.

CHAPTER 3

McGreggor stood looking intently at a map of Idaho and western Montana. He tapped a red grease pencil against his hand but hadn't written anything on the huge laminated map. He stood before it for fifteen minutes. Stood as still as the bronze cowboy on his desk. Only his green eyes moved, darting this way and that, taking in, re-memorizing topography and terrain he'd hiked and hunted hundreds of times, sometimes as a child with his father and brothers, sometimes with Skip and Wally.

Terry was not a tall man, but he was imposing. Where Skip's sheer bulk and ham-fisted-ness made him respected by most, Terry had an air about him that flat scared people, even people who knew him. At first it might have been his haircut, or lack of one. He started losing his hair after graduating Ranger school in the Army. His hair was short then, and it was hardly noticeable. Both his grandfathers were bald and he always figured he didn't stand much of a chance for a ponytail late in life. He had even warned Christina about it before they were married.

He steadfastly refused to comb one of his sideburns over to cover his balding scalp. Instead, he took to shaving his head completely. After he got out of the Army, he let the corners of his mustache creep down an inch, giving him the appearance of a Chinese holyman or a very scary Daddy Warbucks.

When people got close to him though, they realized it wasn't the smooth head or the fumanchu. It was something behind his eyes: an almost complete lack of fear. Terry had come very close to becoming a martial arts master at thirty years of age and as such, he feared no one.

When prisoners acted up or bandits resisted arrest, he dealt with them in a quick dispassionate manner without malice or bravado. He was not mean, but he was not nice either.

Sherry Prather was scared to death of him. Only an inch shorter than Terry, she had curly, strawberry hair, cut just below her ears. She wore a light green flannel shirt with the sleeves rolled up to her elbows and faded jeans, tight enough to accentuate her figure. She was quite attractive, but had an air of confidence about her that scared men off. At least she was normally confident. Terry never said an unkind word to her, quite the opposite. In fact, she never felt able to do a good enough job for him. He was too hard to get a handle on; too hard to talk to. He had the kind of face you tell your kids to stay away from, and he just plain scared her. She wished Skip would get there. Wallace Fuller's death had hit hard. She never knew anyone who met a violent death and she wanted desperately to cry. Somehow, she felt Terry might disapprove of crying though and she struggled to wait until Skip arrived. He was far more approachable.

Knowing Terry would want to see the information she had, she cleared her throat behind him. He turned his head deliberately. She doubted he was ever startled.

"Faxes from Deer Lodge?" He raised an eyebrow.

She nodded and offered him the plain manila folder.

"Thanks Sherry, lets sit down and see what we've got. Skip should be here any minute."

"I'm here now," Skip's deep Texas drawl boomed from the outer office. He walked in and patted Terry on the shoulder. "You okay?" He looked at Sherry.

"Fine," she nodded, though her eyes were moist and there was a tiny, uncontrollable quiver on her chin .

"How about you?" Skip turned to his friend. "Are you alright?"

"I will be. Christina called a few minutes ago." Terry sat at the oval conference table and steepled his hands in front of his face. "The Bishop is over there now. He wants to talk to us as soon we get a lull in the investigation. Christina says he's afraid we have blood on our minds."

"Revenge?" Skip sat in a padded blue chair opposite his friend.

"Apparently." Terry nodded.

"I'd say he's a pretty astute man." Skip picked the top file from the pile on the table and shoved the remaining two to Terry and Sherry respectively. His file was labeled MILLER, Peter.

Pete Miller was born in Denver, Colorado on December 20, 1948. His recorded criminal career began when he was dishonorably discharged from the Marine Corps at age nineteen for severely beating a commanding officer. The vicious act kept him out of Viet Nam but earned him three years in Fort Leavenworth military prison. For a while he tried working at the salvage business but found strong-arm robbery more to his liking. Money was quicker and people rarely argued when a gun was in their face. His rap sheet said his final conviction was for the murder of his father's best friend, a man who helped him buy his first car. The old man was found beside the road shot to death, and Pete was arrested in his car the next day. By all rights he should have gotten the death penalty, but he plead guilty and got life without the possibility of parole.

Skip was not surprised to read a psychological profile stating Miller was a criminal sociopath, very intelligent but devoid of any morals. Killing would come easy to him.

As far as his vital statistics went he was in excellent shape. According to his prison medical he was five feet ten and weighed one hundred seventy pounds. He ate well and had no illnesses worth mentioning. He was an exercise fanatic doing 500 push ups and 100 pull ups every day.

His prison record showed a lengthy history of violence against other inmates. Not the kind of random exercise yard fighting of many inmates, but a cold calculated violence to gain power and influence within the system.

Skip read about several violent incidents in an effort to better learn about his quarry. Across the conference table, Sherry Prather shivered at the thought of a man as bad as James Robert Conklin.

Born in 1974 in Lolo, Montana, little Jimmy Conklin started his brushes with the law before he was a teenager. In juvenile hall more than out before he was eighteen, Conklin spent exactly two and a half months on the street as a legal adult before being arrested for the brutal assault of a sixteen year old neighbor girl. His sentencing judge had dubbed him a predator who did not deserve to see the light of day for at least twenty years.

Terry finished reading the file on Carl Meeks and tossed it across the table to Sherry. "This guy's got an ex wife in Canada. He evidently spent time there some years ago. May still have some contacts."

"I get the feeling from reading Miller's jacket that he wouldn't have invited Carl on this jaunt if he didn't know something about where they were going," Skip said.

Sherry nodded in agreement. "The guy I spoke with at the prison this morning said Miller would definitely be in charge. According to him, the other two are just hangers."

For the next few minutes the only sound in the conference room was the creaking of cheap government furniture and the ruffling of flimsy fax paper. Sherry finished the file on Miller and slid it away from her in disgust as if to distance herself from the man instead of his paperwork. She got up to get herself a cup of coffee. That was one good thing about Skip and Terry; they never expected her to get them coffee. She had never worked around Mormons before and had not known what to think at first. Her parents warned her with all sorts of silly notions about working in the office with two Mormon men and how they would treat her. Apart from the fact that the two men were closer than family to each other, they generally made her feel accepted and part of the team. She possessed common sense, a deep love for the work, and was not a city girl by any rights and that helped considerably.

Terry rose from the table and walked back to the map behind him on the wall. "What's their next move?" he said to himself, scanning the vast country on the map between Missoula and the Canadian border. The Cabinet Mountains are not as tall as some mountains in Montana, but they are just as rough and wild. They stretch in a long jumbled line north west along the Clark Fork River and north along the Idaho border through Libby and Yaak. There, they join the Purcells that sprawl across the Canadian border between the Roosville and Eastport ports of entry.

"Skip," Terry turned to face his friend. "They took Fuller's patrol car and no other vehicles have been reported stolen yet. They can't drive all the way to Canada without getting caught. If they try it on foot out here, without some sort of supplies, they'll never make it." Terry held a measuring string up along the green area between Missoula and the border. "About a hundred and ninety miles as the crow flies."

Skip nodded and twirled the curly end of his mustache. "That's not counting the wandering around they'd do." He walked over to get a closer look at the map and put his finger on Interstate 90 leading west out of Missoula.

"Let's say they're heading north, the easiest thing to do would be stay to the Clark Fork until they get up to Noxon." He followed the blue line of the river with his finger.

"It would," Terry said. "But there's a main road along there. It's pretty well traveled and they're more likely to be spotted. I don't think Miller would risk that. He'll have to know we have road blocks up."

"True," said Sherry from behind them. "Sergeant Jordan told me the Highway Patrol already have roadblocks at St. Regis and the Idaho border. He said they put one up on I 90 east of Missoula as well, in case they doubled back. Sanders county sheriff has 200 blocked at Thompson

Falls and 28 to Hot Springs. They've got as many of the back roads patrolled as they have men for."

"That'll force them to keep to the woods which ever route they take," Skip said, twirling his mustache and studying the topographic lines on the map. "I've got a gut feeling they're going to ground. This is rough country. Meeks has a bum leg and Jimmy Conklin's record doesn't show him to be in any kind of shape to be gallivanting over hill and dell."

"That leaves Miller," said Sherry, who had moved up next to Skip and Terry at the map. The powerful desire to find Fuller's killers was contagious and she found herself wishing she could hunt them as well.

Terry didn't look away from the wall map. "Right. That leaves Miller. The mountains might kill the other two but if anyone can make it through he will."

Skip tore his gaze from the map to look at his watch. "What time is that meeting with the locals?"

"Ten thirty," said Sherry.

"We'd better git then, we only have fifteen minutes."

Terry nodded.

"Keep me informed guys. Would you please?" Sherry said as she picked up her small leather purse.

"You bet." Skip gave her a wry wink and they filed out the door together.

CHAPTER 4

To the dismay of his peers, Lieutenant Carey Forbisher had risen rapidly within the ranks of the Montana Highway Patrol. It had nothing to do with any kind of stellar performance of his duties. In that respect, he didn't quite make it to the average level. The fact was, he was willing to go anywhere and do anything to advance his career. Early on, he had been willing to take the remote, out of the way postings, dragging his wife to Wolf Point on the Fort Peck Indian Reserve to take a corporals position. He made Sergeant by moving back across the state to bleak, dirty Browning. He took tests well and the promotion board in Helena awarded him his Lieutenant bars because of his high scores.

In days past, he hadn't been in such bad shape. The state police were sticklers for fitness and he had once been in relatively good shape. It seemed that lately though, the weight of his high office had pushed his shoulders down around his middle, and he looked more like an upside down ice cream cone than a rough, tough Montana State Trooper. He couldn't seem to find time to exercise with all the paper work. His Sam Browne belt was a good two sizes too small, and he found himself more and more going without a gun completely. Now, the Captain was here from Helena and he had to suck in his belly, wrap the gun belt around him and be in full uniform.

He felt bad for Fuller's wife and kids. It hurt the whole outfit when a brother officer went down, but his stomach hurt from the tight girth of wide leather and it was beginning to show in his disposition. He would have been more than content to let the investigators handle the whole shebang except for the fact that the Captain had arrived. Most of the forces from the western half of the state came to help with roadblocks and other aspects of the manhunt. Sheriff's deputies and local police from all around the Missoula area were either out combing the back country roads or sitting in front of Forbisher at the planning meeting. The pudgy lieutenant stood behind the podium and looked out at all the faces in the meeting room. Fuller was well liked and that accounted for the incredible turnout. It was one thing to have a comrade go down, but it was something else if everyone thought the world of that comrade: if he had helped put a new roof on this one's house, or helped bring in that one's cattle for the fall. Most of these men knew Fuller personally, and many of them had been touched by his generosity. Forbisher found himself wondering how many would show up to help if he was killed. More than half the crowd were strangers to him. He consoled himself by trying to make a good impression on the Captain, but his strangling stomach ached so badly, he was beginning to wish the Captain would just go back to Helena.

Skip and Terry sat next to three investigators from the State Bureau of Narcotics, toward the back at one of the long tables that filled the conference room. The meeting began with each officer standing for introductions and telling how much manpower their respective departments would pledge to the manhunt.

"We are certain they are somewhere in here," said Forbisher, adjusting the roll of fat over his spit-shined belt and drawing a two hundred mile circle with a felt tip marker around the rest area where Fuller was killed.

He spoke more to the slim, grey haired captain who sat to his immediate left than the rest of the group, as if he was the only one of any importance in the room. "There hasn't been any activity on the roads this morning and Trooper Fuller's vehicle has not yet been located. We have roadblocks at every intersection leading away from the crime scene. It doesn't matter which way they went, when they make another move, we'll find them."

"Has anyone talked to Meeks' contacts in Canada?" Terry asked from the back of the room.

Forbisher nodded. "RCMP are looking into that now, but these men will never make it that far, I promise you. When they ditch the patrol car, they will need another vehicle. If they steal one, we'll find out about it and be right there, on top of them so fast their heads will spin."

"What if they try to walk out?" Terry tipped his chair onto the back legs.

Forbisher didn't like answering questions in front of his superior, and he glared at the deputy. "We have six planes and three helicopters in the air over the mountains between here and Canada as well as a news helicopter from as far away as Channel Two in Spokane who want an exclusive when we catch these guys. It's a long way to walk to the border and those mountains are brutal. If they try to walk out and do somehow slip past us, which they won't, the terrain will kill 'em. Some elk hunter will find their bones in a few months."

"I'd just as soon find them myself, I've got some things I would like to say to them," Skip muttered, loud enough for everyone to hear. A resounding murmur of agreement carried around the room.

The lieutenant held up a pale, chubby hand. "I know everyone's got blood on their minds. That's natural. Just remember what we are all about."

"And remember the news helicopters and their eye in the sky," shot the chief deputy from Missoula county. "We don't need anything untoward being broadcast on the evening edition."

"That's right," said Forbisher. "Look, I would like nothing more than to saddle a horse and lead you all on a wild posse ride through the mountains," he lied. "Trust me though. These men are going to come out on a road, and when they do we will catch them. They have to eat and they have to have shelter. This is not the wild west."

With that he picked up a stack of papers from the podium and enlisted officers from the front two rows to help him pass them around the room.

"We'll stay in communication through our channel and the respective frequency of which ever county you happen to be operating. Each individual Sheriff is responsible for manning the roadblocks in their own county. The rest of you maintain patrol of the quadrants I've outlined in the packets. Those agencies not specifically mentioned, can play it however they wish. We'll put out a signal on all frequencies when any contact is made or new evidence is obtained."

Skip thumbed through his packet. It was a good half an inch thick and filled with maps of the area and manpower assignment charts. "It's no wonder he's fat," Skip whispered to Terry. "He has a man down, and the first thing he does is sit down at his computer and write a book." Those within earshot chuckled. No one in particular liked Forbisher.

The United States Marshals were not mentioned in Forbisher's ops plan so Terry and Skip excused themselves quickly after the meeting. Everyone knew they were closer to Wally than anyone; some felt they were too close to be part of the investigation. Before anyone could tell them so, they went back to their office to come up with some kind of plan of their own … and wait.

By two that afternoon Skip had broken every yellow number 2 pencil in the office into tiny splinters. The meeting with the state had seemed unfruitful. Everyone was torn up over the death of a brother officer, but there were so few leads to follow. All involved, including Skip wanted to do something, even if it was wrong.

CHAPTER 5
Sunday

Wayne Wheeler was not a bad man. He was a weak man, and, being weak, sometimes he did bad things. He reminded Skip of an Australian Shepherd he'd once owned. It never would come up and bite a person head on, preferring instead to slink around and get a chunk of calf muscle when no one was looking.

Wayne spent the morning arguing with Brother Harden during Priesthood and the last hour trying to prove Sister Watson wrong at every turn during Sunday School class. Now, he sat two rows in back of Skip with his arm along the pew behind Kate Beebe. She moved as far left as she could, but had run out of bench. Wayne didn't exactly have his arm around her. He was pretty sure she wouldn't have let that happen, but it gave the impression he did, and he wanted to make sure Skip took note.

At twenty nine, Wheeler's curly black hair was beginning to thin, and he blamed that for his inability to attract a wife. In truth, it was his sour disposition and sheer lack of character that made him unappealing. He tried in vain to be a dapper dresser but no matter what he wore, his shallow blue eyes and pallid countenance gave the impression of a wrung out dish rag.

He knew Skip had been seeing Kate off and on for weeks and that was precisely the reason he flopped down next to her just before the opening hymn. Skip missed the earlier meetings and came in late to Sacrament with Terry and his family. Wheeler shot him a wry glance and even screwed up enough courage to wink at the much larger man. Skip smiled back at him with a nod, annoyed but too tired to care much about who was sitting by Kate.

Pushing her youngest boy's diaper bag under the pew, Christina leaned over to Skip and whispered, "I wonder if he knows who he's dealing with."

Terry snickered. "He knows exactly what he is doing. He's just not doing it very well."

Skip smiled, noticing how nice Kate's auburn hair looked tucked into tortoise shell combs.

"Maybe we should have set him up with Brenda," Christina leaned over and whispered.

"Shhh!" Terry's six year old, Zane chastised his elders with a toothy grin of righteous indignation.

Christina folded her arms piously. Terry nodded and gave the boy's thigh a squeeze.

Kate Beebe was smart enough not to pay much attention to what Wayne Wheeler was doing. People like him thrived on attention. She saw the same thing every day in her eighth graders. Instead of worrying about the arm around her shoulders she looked at the back of Skip's head and thought of him, two rows ahead of her.

She hadn't known him long, if you considered the grand scheme of things. He had only been in Montana three years and in her ward half of that. She'd heard about him before they met from some of the other sisters at the stake singles' activities.

"He's Garth Brooks meets Batman," winked Pam Reed. "Some sort of cowboy policeman."

"Tall, strong and handsome … and he's moving into your ward," redheaded Laura Peterson grinned. Although single herself, she felt it her sworn duty to find Kate a husband.

"Too good to be true." Kate said, ladling punch into paper cups. "If he's that good he'd be married already."

Sister Reed raised her dark eyebrows up and down and took a conspiratorial tone. "He is, but not for long. His wife hates Montana and from the sounds of it, him too."

"Stupid woman," said Sister Peterson.

"Did it ever occur to you that she may know something you don't know? A chink in his shining armor perhaps?" Kate said as she looked around the room at the other singles. A few danced but most stood huddled in small groups. Men talked to each other about whatever men talk about, and the women talked about … Skip Garret.

Everywhere she turned that evening his name came up. It was common knowledge his wife was returning to Texas, and a divorce was

26

nearly final. He had a good job, something to do with law enforcement, although no one knew for sure, and he was a returned missionary.

"I hear he's gone a lot and his wife didn't like it," said Karen Sharp an attractive brunette from the University Ward.

"That's more like it. He does have a shortcoming or two."

"It's not his fault, his job keeps him gone some," Laura Peterson said twirling a copper lock of hair.

Sister Reed smoothed the front of her denim skirt brushing off some chocolate chip cookie crumbs. "Well, whatever the reason, he is about to be single and he deserves a looking at."

Kate first saw him when he visited church with the McGreggors. She didn't see him come in, but noticed him in Sunday School class. He was tall, with close cropped dirty blond hair, raw boned with wide strong hands and shoulders to match. He had a huge brown mustache that curled up on either side of a hidden upper lip. Besides his mustache, she noticed two other things. His high heeled boots were polished to a high ebony gloss but a little flake of horse manure still clung to the back of one heel and he 'hat hair.' Even though he kept his hair short, the noticeable ring and tiny rooster tail of wayward hair told the world he wore a hat. He made no attempt to comb it out or brush it away. He was dressed fashionably in a starched white shirt and a dark grey suit with a slight western cut. Skip Garret reminded Kate of her father, and in her estimation, those were some pretty large boots to fill.

Now she looked up at him a few rows ahead of her and smiled at the back of his head. He still had hat hair, and he still sat with the McGreggors.

This thing with Brother Fuller scared her. She admitted to herself that she possessed strong feelings for Skip, and she couldn't help but think it could have been him out there dead in the street. She was twenty seven and wanted to have children, maybe even Skip's children, but the thought of those children growing up without a father terrified her. She knew what he did was dangerous, but Brother Fuller's death hammered home an awful reality.

At the same time, it put a tiny doubt in her heart. A doubt that made her wonder if Sister Garret Number One had not been able to put up with the late nights of worry. What if Brenda had not been able to bear up under the stress of wondering if her husband was coming home for dinner or dead at the hand of some homicidal maniac? It was a tiny doubt, but a doubt never the less, and it told her she might not be cut out to be Sister Garret Number Two.

Fuller's death was the main topic of conversation during the meetings of the day. Bishop Morrison asked everyone to keep Tracy and the boys in their prayers and announced that the Relief Society would be providing meals for the next week. He spoke briefly about Wally and the kind of man and father he was. Christina cried quietly as he talked while Terry held her hand in his lap, patting it softly. Skip sat alone, trying to quell the rising anger in his gut.

He chided himself for having such harsh feelings in church. He felt for Tracy and the boys, and he was glad for the show of support from the ward. But, as the Bishop spoke, all he could think of was vengeance. For a brief instant, he transferred that feeling toward Wayne Wheeler but caught himself, not wanting to waste any malice on one so weak.

By the time the Sacrament was passed Skip was in such a inward furry he abstained, passing the tray to little Zane who glowingly took it to his mother and two little brothers. Terry took a piece of bread and handed the tray to the waiting Deacon. Reaching around his wife and children, he squeezed Skip's shoulder.

Many times the three lawmen, had talked late into the night about their feelings regarding spirituality and their chosen profession. Wally had probably said it best.

"The more highly trained you are as an officer and the more you have experienced, the less comfortable the good members of the church are when they have to be around you," he observed one night while they sat around a woodstove in elk camp. "Do you suppose anyone was ever really at ease around Porter Rockwell or Captain Moroni? Dangerous men always have an element of danger about them." Wally said, sticking another length of tamarack into the glowing stove. "Even if we are the good guys, we tend to scare people."

They had known he was right. Rather than argue, the three commiserated the peculiarities people in law enforcement tend to share with one another.

Terry and Skip were headliners on the local news that week for a particularly violent arrest and had become keenly aware of how standoffish the people at church could be the following Sunday. The local television station played up the fact that Terry broke a man's arm during the raid and Skip smashed in another rowdy's face with a glass ashtray. Of course, the reporter didn't spend much time on the fact that the man Terry wounded was armed with a shotgun and would likely have killed somebody had he not been so discouraged by a dangling arm. They also forgot to mention that the outlaw who caught the ashtray in the mouth was hiding in the closet with a knife and could consider himself extremely lucky Skip hadn't shot him.

Terry swore Sister Kellog yanked her children out of the way when he walked past them in the hall, but Christina said he was just imagining things.

Fuller was a great smiler. Older than Terry and Skip by ten years, he was used to such behavior and took it in stride most of the time. He grinned at Terry and rubbed the top of his bald head; something few people had leave to do. "None of these good brothers and sisters would have wanted to have those guys selling dope to their kids. They are surely glad to have them off the street. It's a little distasteful to them to think of sitting next to the type of man who could break a mans limbs or knock his teeth out with an ashtray one day and then show up to teach the deacons quorum the next."

Wally was the philosopher of the three.

The youth speaker, a shy young Beehive with freckles across her nose, unfolded a piece of paper that had been ripped from a spiral notebook, and smoothed it out on the podium. She was at the age where she insisted on fixing her own hair for church but hadn't yet practiced enough to get it exactly right. Pushing a blond lock out of her eyes, she glanced up at the crowd. Skip saw her looking directly at him and gave her a playful wink. Blushing, she started in on her talk.

Skip turned for a moment to look at Kate. She smiled faintly. That is, her mouth smiled but her wide, green eyes were puffy and moist. Her tired gaze lingered on Skip's face for a moment, as if she was making some final, well thought out decision. Wayne Wheeler patted her on the shoulder with a pale, bony hand and then looked at Skip to make sure he noticed.

The remainder of the meeting went quickly, with another youth speaker and a visiting high councilman speaking on subjects that were surely recorded in heaven but were lost on the ears of Skip and Terry. Skip fumbled with a gold pocket watch, a going away gift from his friends at the Ft. Worth Police Department, and let his mind drift. He wondered why Kate had given him that peculiar look.

Terry sat with Colton in his lap, watching the four year old color a picture of a pioneer. When he was bored with that, Terry let the boy pretend his thumbs were a milk cow and whiled away the time.

Once the meeting was over, Skip was happy to see Kate gather her purse and get quickly to her feet. Wheeler busied himself talking to another group of people in the aisle. Kate smiled again but the flow of people leaving pushed her out into the lobby.

Skip helped Christina pick up the scattered crayons and stray Cheerios and they all walked out together.

CHAPTER 6

The weather was cool outside and much more comfortable to visit in than stuffy halls. The building was going on its second set of meetings for the day and needed a good airing. Pockets of people stood here and there between the double glass doors to the lobby and the main parking lot. Groups of children played tag on the well mown grass, some of them roughhousing under the wide canopy of a huge weeping birch. It was three-thirty and the hazy, orange rays of the sun gave the area a cozy appeal. A few insects, backlit by the glow, hung in scant swarms, holding on to the last few hours of summer. The gentle breeze seemed to whisper, 'enjoy this now, winter will be here in no time.'

A scruffy young Deacon with a tie long enough to be his father's and a huge grass stain along one arm of his white shirt had a much larger boy with glasses by the wrist. He lit up when he saw Terry come out the doors with his family.

"Brother McGreggor, can you show me how to do this wrist throw the right way?"

Terry, ever the teacher, stepped in next to the two boys. The young men, always hungry for martial arts instruction, flocked to him like disciples when he was around. "It's the Sabbath," he said with a frown. When Terry frowned a person took notice and the deacon became wide eyed. "I don't think this is the kind of activity the Lord wants us to do on His day. Do you?" He took the larger boy by the wrist and motioned with his other hand for the Deacon to watch. "However, since I won't be seeing you for a few days and you are likely to tear out your big brother's shoulder, if you're not careful, I'll show you now, but you have to promise to practice it tomorrow."

"Sure!" said both boys at once, and a small crowd of Aaronic Priesthood gathered around to receive instruction.

Brother Grant, a red bearded, barrel of a man stopped to watch on the way to his truck. Actually, very quiet and timid, his big chest and strong hands belied his demeanor. The thought of a law enforcement job at once interested and scared him. He had spoken with Terry about it a few times but never in depth. Fascinated by the fluid movements, he watched Terry turn the deacons in smooth arcs forcing them without effort to yield to his throws and joint locks.

He was twenty three and old enough to know better, but he asked anyway. "Have you ever killed anyone?" As soon as he said the words, he felt stupid.

Terry placed the Deacon's hand on his own wrist, showing him proper technique and glanced up at brother Grant, his eyes narrow and menacing. "Why? Do you need me to kill somebody for you?"

The effect was like stomping a foot at a timid dog. Brother Grant blustered and said, "Why, no I just meant … never mind. Have a good Sunday. Sorry about Wally." He walked quickly to his truck without looking back and drove away.

Skip stood watching, a hand in his pocket and a brown wool blazer thrown over his shoulder. He shook his head and chuckled under his breath. That was the question people always asked. Normally, he and Terry would politely refuse an answer, but the past events had put everyone on edge.

Loosening his tie, Skip rolled his sleeves up to the forearm to enjoy the cool air even more. A soft padding in the grass caused him to turn and he found himself looking at Kate. As always, she looked beautiful. Her auburn hair hung down past strong shoulders, even with the sides up in combs. Her cheeks were pink and healthy from the cool breeze. She used little make up, just a touch around the eyes and Skip chided her for even that. She wore a dark green knee length skirt and a fuzzy pink angora sweater. Her canvas bag was full of scriptures and lesson materials for her primary class. Just a few inches shorter than Skip, she had played basketball in college and still retained her athletic figure.

"Have you got a minute?" She asked.

"You bet. I was sort of hoping to get you away from Wayne." Skip grinned and took the book bag while they walked together toward the softball field.

After a few steps and no words, Kate stopped and stared across the field of wheat-stubble behind the chapel. Running her fingers through thick, cinnamon hair, she let it fall slowly across the nape of her pale neck, orange in the hazy evening light. The fluid grace and beauty of the movement, while obvious to everyone around her, was completely lost on Kate Beebe.

Where Brenda had been so self-aware, spending hours in front of a mirror to get her hair just right, a puff of breeze and a toss of her head were usually enough to leave Kate perfectly styled.

"I was so sorry to hear about Wally." Her voice was hushed and cracking. In an attempt to regain control of herself she walked again.

"Me too … me too."

Her Plymouth was at the very end of the parking lot beside the ball field, and she stopped when she got to it. "Listen," she said. "I know you are busy with this thing, but I wanted to tell how bad I felt. I feel so bad for Tracy …" Her green eyes were fast welling up with tears. Skip started to say something to comfort her, but she put a fingertip to his lips. "I don't think I could handle what she's going through. Do you know what I mean?"

Skip took a red bandanna out of his hip pocket and gave it to her. "I think you could handle a lot more than you think you could."

"You know I worry about you every day as it is. I sometimes forget what I'm teaching, I start to think about you so hard."

"I'll bet the kids think that's pretty funny."

"They're eighth graders. They aren't listening to much I say anyway." She dabbed at her eyes with the bandanna. "I'm serious though. I get sick to my stomach when I think about you going after these men."

"I'll be fine. I have Terry there to protect me." Skip gestured to the weeping birch.

Kate smiled, but her eyes seemed glazed. "Yes, I see he is letting the Deacons beat him up again." Terry had just allowed the Deacon with the long tie to throw him to the grass. "I feel much better now." She scuffed at the grass with the toe of her black pump.

"Can I ask you something?"

"Sure."

Wayne Wheeler had parked his gold Pontiac Firebird next to Kate and was now standing by the door. "Hey Kate, see you at the singles dance?" He spoke to Kate but kept a beady eye on Skip.

"I don't know Wayne. I'll have to see how I feel after school on Friday." She was going to have to talk to the Bishop about her calling as Single Adult Rep.

Skip stood beside Kate but didn't speak. He considered Wheeler more of a nuisance than a threat. Still, the man had interrupted a private conversation and could only be allowed a certain amount of that sort of latitude. Skip gave his best 'get out of here we have something to talk about' look, but Wheeler was apparently too dense to get the message.

"Are you doing anything after church today?" Wheeler dropped his books on the front seat of his car and shut the door; a sure sign he did not intend to leave any time soon.

The best thing to do with weeds like this was to nip them off early and at the root. "She was talking to me," said Skip unfolding his arms and standing up from the fender. He was four inches taller than the rumpled man, but his silver-belly hat and Wheeler's slouchy attitude made the difference seem much greater.

Deep inside, Wheeler himself knew he didn't care that much for Kate. He just disliked Skip and Terry, and he had made a grave error in thinking he was safer picking at Skip. Terry petrified him and the thought of even speaking to him made Wheeler panic. He had no way of knowing that Terry's martial arts training made him lethal but less prone to fits of temper. In the grand scheme of things Skip was more unstable and therefore much more dangerous.

But, to Wayne Wheeler, Skip seemed a hick and because of that, vulnerable. "You know Skippie, you should come to the singles dance too. We play a little country music. I'm sure we'd all get a kick out of your big Texas hat."

Kate caught the spark of emotion that was in Skip's eye and patted his arm. He gave her a wink and took a step closer to the other man.

Skip's voice was calm and slow, his west Texas drawl heightening its effect. "I'll tell you one thing Brother, if you ever call me 'Skippie' again you'll get a kick out my big Texas boots."

Kate stifled a grin behind Skip's bandanna, and Wheeler scampered back to his car. Once he was inside, he felt relatively safe. "See you Friday Kate," he said.

"He's a cur dog. You know that don't you?" Skip said after Wheeler drove away. "I'll have to inform him of the ten foot rule."

"The ten foot rule?" Kate was puzzled.

"Yeah, as long as he stays at least ten feet away form me, I won't kick his butt."

She handed him back his damp bandanna. "Now Skippie."

Skip narrowed an eye and grinned. "What were you about to ask me when Brother Cur Dog showed up?"

33

Kate looked down at the ground, gathering her thoughts. "Well you don't have to tell me if you don't want to … but I was wondering … why do you think Brenda left you? Was it something like this … that she worried all the time?"

Skip shook his head with a disgusted laugh. "Heavens no. I suppose she did worry about me now and then. Still does I imagine. We are still … I guess you could even call us friends."

"What was it then?" She stared up into his eyes. He could tell she not only wanted, but needed an answer.

"The truth?"

Kate shrugged. "If you don't mind."

Garret chuckled softly to himself and squatted down to pick up an errant pine cone that had found its way to the softball field. He fumbled with it absent mindedly and looked up at Kate's soft green eyes. Her face was passive and she seemed prepared to wait all evening for her answer.

"I've thought about this a lot," Skip said, standing to throw the pine cone far across the parking lot. "Lost a considerable amount of sleep over it as a matter of fact. I could tell you some of my theories. She didn't really know me when we got married. And later, when she found out who I am, I wasn't what she wanted. I don't know, she said the job came between us, but I think she would have run off if I worked at the post office and came home every night at six. Fact is, she probably would have left me sooner if she had to put up with me that much."

Skip sighed and took off his hat to run a hand through his hair. "The truth is, it all comes down to this … I believe a man should still be able to pee off his own back porch."

Kate tittered in mock embarrassment. "Pardon?"

"I need the country, Kate. I love the smell of a horse corral and all that goes with it. I honestly tried to change for her, but when I did, she liked me even less. I guess it's just as simple as that. Brenda wanted to live near a big city and have block parties with all our neighbors. I wanted to live where the neighbors were far enough away that I could …"

Kate's eyes sparkled with mischief. "Pee off your own back porch."

He tilted his hat back and nodded. "Exactly. Although it doesn't sound as sensible when you say it."

They walked for a while, taking a turn around the softball field, saying nothing. When they got back to her car, Skip said, "I'm apt to be pretty busy the next few days. Still, I hate to think about you at that dance with Brother Weasel." He was well passed the beating around the bush stage of his life. "I know it's hard dating, let alone getting serious with a man like me."

"I'd like to think I'm up to the task." Kate looked into his eyes and saw a softness there, a softness not many got to see. He had only kissed her once. She had been out riding with him at his place. Cowboy to the bone, he was all manners and yes ma'ams— he still took his hat off when he spoke to her. Helping her down from the saddle, even though she hadn't needed it, he stole a kiss. There had been a pause, but not an awkward one and although their relationship had changed from that moment, they had not spoken of it again.

She opened her car door and took her book bag. "You come by when you have time. I'll make you supper." Her heart was racing from being so near to him; racing she feared, to try and outrun the tiny but nagging doubts about their relationship. Not about Skip or the kind of man he was, but doubts about whether she could handle the life she seemed hopelessly headed for. Things seemed so out of control. Kate was certain she wasn't going to be able to make any rational decisions standing there looking into his soft, blue eyes, with his hat tipped back in that boyish way of his. Shaking her head, she kissed him softly on the cheek and climbed into her car.

Skip laughed at himself and rubbed the spot where she kissed him. He knew it was silly, but he couldn't help wishing Wayne Wheeler had been there to see it.

Watching the back of Kate's head as she drove away, he walked slowly across the almost empty parking lot. As much as he loved Brenda while they were married, he could not remember a time when he watched the back of her head and had such fond feelings. He shrugged off the philosophical thoughts. It made his stomach hurt to think of Kate and Brenda at the same time.

Crossing the chapel lawn to where the last of the Deacon's parents rescued them from Terry, Skip picked up a birch switch to defend himself. Little Zane, armed with a long stick was pretending to be Zorro. Christina still stood at the doors to the lobby talking primary business with a baby on her hip and Colton clutching the calf of her leg.

"Who's tougher Mr. Skip?" Zane asked with a raised eyebrow and a flourish of his birch sword. "Zorro or the Power Rangers?"

"No question Zaniac. Zorro." Skip had to move fast to block the six year old's slashes and thrusts.

Zane held his stick steady at Skip's chest and scratched his tousled blonde hair. "How do you know that?"

"Well, look at this way. Does Zorro need a dinosaur?"

"Nope, but he has a horse." Zane said, preparing to run him through.

Skip held up a hand. "Hold on there. Does Zorro need four or five other heroes to help him out all the time?"

Zane let the tip of his stick dip to the ground and shook his head. "Nuh uh. I guess not." The boy grinned and raised his stick again as quickly as it he let it drop. "Prepare for the mark of the Z, you puny Power Ranger." Attacking with the fury that earned him the nick name Zaniac, the boy whipped and slashed with his birch sword. He saw the patrol car before anyone else.

"Police, Police!" Zane cried, smiling and waving his stick franticly toward the road.

Skip and Terry who both had their backs to the street, turned in time to see a Missoula County patrol unit pull into the parking lot. Both knew Rueben Salt, the big Indian deputy driving the squad. They had all worked together on several fugitive cases. He didn't get out of the car, motioning instead for the two marshals to come to him. He was a nice enough person, but he was shy and churches scared him—too many good folks. Rueben preferred crowds of people he knew needed arresting, so he kept to the safety of his patrol car.

"Hey Rueben." Terry rolled his sleeves back down from the lesson. Skip was right behind him.

"Hey boys." The sheriff's deputy waited for the two to get close enough for others not to hear. He could see Christina studying him from across the parking lot and waved at her politely with short, chubby fingers.

"What's up?" Skip asked, leaning over to shake the deputy's hand through the window.

"I got some news I thought you guys would be interested in. I know how close you were to Fuller." Salt was more than a little over weight, and his round cheeks gave the impression he was grinning even when he wasn't. Even now, as he spoke of a fallen friend his eyes held a hint of mischief. "I just got back from the coroner's office."

Skip stiffened. The thought of an autopsy on Wallace appalled him. He knew it would be done, but he had witnessed too many and the brutal idea of it interrupted the soft feelings he was having about Kate.

Terry was more practical. "So what did you find out?" He wiped sweat from his forehead.

Reaching across the seat of his patrol car with a grunt, Rueben retrieved a clear plastic bag sealed with red evidence tape, and held it up to the window.

"Looks like teeth," Terry said, taking the bag for closer inspection.

Inside the small bag were two teeth, an incisor and a canine. Both were human. The incisor was whole with the root still attached. The canine was broken off above the root and looked to have part of a filling with it.

Terry handed the bag to Skip for his examination. "Who's are they?"

"That's the good part," said Rueben. "Doc dug them out of Fuller's knuckles. Looks like he put up a hell of a fight. Make's you feel a little better knowing he got a piece of the guys that jumped him, don't it?"

"Yes," Skip said, giving the officer back the bag. "Yes it does. But not near as good as I'll feel when I can meet the man who owns those teeth."

"You're right about that my friend," agreed Terry. He looked across the parking lot toward his little family and thought of Wally Fuller's wife and two sons. "You are right about that."

CHAPTER 7

The Sloans moved to their mining claim on Trestle Creek because they enjoyed being alone. Harvey staked the claim when he was barely twenty and was working as a lumberjack in the later part of 1937. Rose had been camp cook. Being the only woman in a lumber camp was a tough row to hoe, but she handled it with grace and flair. At twenty three, she was older than many of the boys in camp and acted not only as cook, but as nurse and surrogate mother. Nearly all the young loggers harbored tender feelings for her. Some were more than a thousand miles from their own mothers and sweethearts but they acted like gentlemen and treated her with respect.

On Saturday nights, the lumber boss hosted a dance, and each man dutifully waited his turn to dance with the flaxen haired Rose. She swore to herself she wouldn't get attached to anyone in particular so loved them all like brothers, until Harvey Sloan came along. He was quiet and strong and had a vision. The other men didn't have that vision-look. Harvey didn't talk much, but his love for the mountains sprang like fire in his deep blue eyes.

To the consternation, and considerable disappointment, of sixteen other lumberjacks, Rose chose Harvey to marry. She continued to cook and he continued to cut trees but in the mean time he also made a respectable nest egg from his gold gleanings. Never enough to get rich, but enough to build a nice cabin. After a stint in the Pacific during World War II, they started a small outfitting and guide service and ran it out of the ranch next to his old mining claim.

Neither Harvey nor Rose cared much for civilization. The handful of dudes they took into the mountains each year on sightseeing and hunting trips, provided them with all the socializing they needed. They had no television, and although they did own a radio, they seldom turned it on. Harvey preferred Rose's singing to anyone else's, and the news rarely affected him way up in his woods. Deer and elk, along with the riding stock, provided plenty of entertainment. He could never understand what the flatlanders saw in television.

Pitching a fork full of hay over the rail fence into the wooden feeder, Harvey watched a plump, rat tailed Appaloosa munch a mouth full. The horse had a contented look in his eye, as if it was just happy to be alive on such a mountain crisp autumn evening. At seventy plus-years, it took Harvey longer to get the evening feeding done. He didn't care though, he took pleasure in caring for his animals and tending to their needs.

It was dusk by the time he threw the last fork of hay and dumped the final scoop of grain. Rose happened to be in Superior visiting her sister, so there was no reason to hurry inside. Instead, he leaned on his pitch fork handle, watching his animals eat and enjoying the brisk mountain air. The singing gurgle of the creek above the barn was all the music he needed when Rose was away.

Rudy, a bi-eyed husky stood next to him, giving the darkening woods above the corrals a once over with an intense stare from his mottled brown and blue eyes. A low growl rattled deep in his chest.

Harvey rubbed his old friend on the head and looked in the same direction. "Whatcha got boy? A lion?" Rose made a big fuss when she saw a cougar the week before stalking one of mule colts. She had taken a shot but missed. Harvey accused her of missing on purpose; she was getting soft hearted in her old age.

The dog's growl grew more intense. Eyes glued to the black tree-line, his lips curled back revealing shiny white fangs, and the mane of grey and white fur bristled on his neck. Harvey began to feel uneasy himself. Unable to contain himself any longer, Rudy let loose a high pitched bark and darted through the corral into the woods. An instant after the dog hit the woods, Harvey heard the loud boom of a shot, then a quiet, pitiful yelp. A hunter, the old man thought. A hunter had killed his dog! Anger at the thought of it made his head shake. He wanted to cry out but before he could make a sound, dust from a dozen pellets kicked up at his feet and he heard another shot.

Whoever shot Rudy was now shooting at him.

With a swiftness that belied his seventy-six years, Harvey dropped his pitchfork and rolled under the rail fence into the crowded corral. Whoever it was must be a horrible shot, he thought to himself, if they couldn't even hit an old man leaning on a pitchfork. Ducking behind a hay bunk, he narrowly escaped another barrage of buckshot as it ripped into the side of the wood planked trough.

Sloan's antics combined with the shooting alarmed the horses and they milled about in their small enclosure. Tails flagging in the air and steamy vapor coming from their noses, they snorted and ran from one end of the corral to the other. One of the mules, the one Rose called Comet, began to bray loudly, its rasping wheezes echoing off the mountain side. Another shot boomed out from the direction of the trees kicking up dirt and manure a few feet to Harvey's left. The gathering darkness made it hard for him to see but it also was saving his life. Whoever was shooting could have easily hit him with more light.

The old man surveyed his situation. He had not survived over sixty years in these mountains by having slow or poor reactions to danger. Gathering darkness, along with seven horses and four mules gave him cover for the moment. The barn was more than twenty five feet away from the hay bunk and across open ground. The house, where he kept his gun, was too far and out of the question. As spry as Harvey was, he could never hope to outrun the buckshot being fired from the trees.

The creek ran through the middle of the corral and he entertained the fleeting notion of crawling to it and trying to float away in the twilight. He had read a story about a great great grandfather of his who escaped from the Blackfoot that way. The air was chilly though, and at his age he didn't figure he'd survive the frigid water long enough to get off his own property.

Two minutes ticked slowly by without any more shots. The horses and mules, accustomed to a certain amount of gun fire, gathered around their hay-bunk again and started to eat. They were used to Sloan too, and although he had never laid down for a nap beside their feed bunk, payed little attention to the old man at their feet.

Without lifting his head from the familiar-smelling dirt and manure-covered ground, Sloan decided to negotiate. He was well beyond trying to second guess human nature but maybe this was some sort of mistake. He could not for the life of him figure why anyone would be shooting at him.

"Hey!" he yelled. Expecting another barrage of buckshot, he pressed his face into the damp soil and tried to flatten even further against the ground. He was dressed in insulated coveralls, but he began to shiver. "Whatcha shooting at me for?"

Only the sound of the animals chewing cut the silence and Harvey could feel his heart digging a hole in the ground under his chest. Then a voice, muffled but clear enough to understand, came from the black line of trees.

"For starters you can stay still long enough for me to kill ya." There was a sneer in the voice and Harvey made it out to be that of a younger man. "Where did your friend go?"

"Friend?" Harvey kept his face down and strained to hear movement. His brain raced, trying to figure out who the voice was talking about.

"That old cobb with the long hair. You two might as well give it up."

"Nobody here but me, son," Harvey said, shaking his head in the cool dirt. Not only was he pinned down by a dog killing gunman, but a crazy, or cross eyed, gunman to boot.

"Whatever you say, old man. I know yur wife's a good shot or I'd have just walked up and got ya earlier. No worries though, my friends'll be taking care of her any minute now."

Harvey's throat tightened, gripped by a moment of panic before he remembered Rose was at her sister's. He'd have to do something soon. This shooter's friends were sure to know soon that Rose was not home and they would just stroll up and shoot him like a wounded deer.

Joe, the rat tailed appy nosed him gently on the shoulder. Harvey could feel warm breath on the back of his neck and smell the sweet scent of chewed hay. The horse had been born on the Sloan place eighteen years before and became Harvey's favorite trail horse before he was a three year old. They'd gone many miles together. The old Appaloosa knew the trails better than Harvey. Short enough for the old man to get on and off of even at his age, Joe was almost as wide as he was long. More roan than anything, with a orange stub of a tail, the color of a peeled carrot, and a wild mane that stuck straight up like a zebra's.

Harvey Sloan looked up at the sleepy eyes and decided what he'd do. He clucked softly as he had done a thousand times over the last eighteen years each time he fed or handled the animal. The Appaloosa lowered his head and nibbled the denim collar of the man's coveralls with a mottled pink upper lip. Harvey petted with his right hand, working up and around the hard, round curve of the horse's boney jaw and over the top of its head. Enjoying a welcome scratch behind the ears, the animal closed his eyes and hung his head almost to the ground.

With his fingers woven tightly through a handful of mane, Harvey hauled his body into a sitting position, just managing to grab another wad of mane with his left hand before the startled horse could pull its head away.

Wrapping his left hand around a thick hank of mane, he hung on with all his might. The Appaloosa, frightened at the sudden movement, jerked its head back and the old man was yanked to his feet. When the horse turned to get away, Harvey kicked it square in the belly. When he was a young man, Harvey and his brother would show off for the girls in Lolo with this same trick, but now his legs, once used to hours of mountain hiking, were turning to rubber and he knew he had to move quickly or risk a heart attack. Running along side the trotting animal, Harvey felt as if his lungs would explode.

Giving his best war whoop, he gave Joe another swift kick in his fat belly, urging him to lunge forward into a lope. It nearly tore his old shoulders from their sockets, but the transition of gaits jerked the man like a rag doll onto the horse's broad back. Bending low and gripping the horse's mane, Harvey hung on with his legs and pointed the horse for the far end of the corral.

He had taken enough dudes hunting to know they all had trouble hitting anything running on the diagonal. Aiming the Appaloosa at the lowest spot in the fence, he dug in with heels. Leaning forward, he whispered words of encouragement into the animal's ear. Falling off now would leave him in the open, as well as break most of his bones on the rocky ground. As experienced a rider as he was, if the horse refused or shied at the fence, Harvey knew he wouldn't be able to stay on without a saddle.

Buckshot whistled over his back and a string of high pitched rifle shots whined by in the darkness. The second volley came from the direction of the house. Harvey said a silent prayer of thanks that Rose was away.

Nostrils flaring and stub tail flagging in excitement, Joe thundered across the last few feet of the corral. The Appaloosa was old, but not too old to jump a four-rail corral fence. More shots rang out and men's voices could be heard cursing when he sailed across the top rail. Horse and rider hit with a thud on the hard packed ground outside the fence. Harvey was thrown forward onto the horses neck, but curled his toes underneath the animal's belly and hung fast.

Not giving the animal a chance to think for itself, the old man dug in harder with his heels and headed toward the trail at the west end of his place. He stayed in a crouch, fearing a low branch in the darkness as much as a bullet. Guiding with his knees, he disappeared into the forest and didn't slow for two miles until he had reached a main logging road off the mountain.

Jim Conklin threw the shotgun to the ground when the fat Appaloosa disappeared into the dark shadows of the forest. Every shot from the twelve gauge rattled his aching head and jaw. He would never have admitted it to the others, but after the first round his head was hurting so badly, tears streamed down his face and made any sort of accurate shooting impossible. He swore, that through blurred vision he had seen two old men in the corrals. He tried to rub the bloody haze from his eyes after he fired the first shots, and when he did, one old man vanished from his sight. He put it down as a simple case of double vision—but the second old man seemed to look different—he had a flowing white beard and long, silver grey hair. The image quickly slipped from his memory as Conklin turned his attention to his hurting head.

Miller stood beside the open door to the Sloan's cabin and shook his head in disgust. He'd hoped for a night's rest in a comfortable bed. But now, with the old man getting away, the law was bound to come raining down by morning, if not before. It would take the old man a little while to get off the mountain to a phone, and that would give them just enough time to get something to eat and gather up a few supplies for the trail.

Pete waved the other two men into the house. He tucked the trooper's pistol into his waistband and looked up at the night sky. Heavy clouds rolled in from the north and obscured the stars. That meant nothing to guide them until morning. From the looks of the gathering storm it meant a lot of rain. It would cover their tracks but would also make things uncomfortable. Peter Miller hated to be uncomfortable. Jimmy Conklin was to blame for this. He let the old man get away, and he would pay when the time was right.

Carl was the first inside the cabin and he flopped down on the small brocade love seat in the living room, his double chin resting sullenly on his chest. The bad knee pained him fiercely and he had been unable to walk without a noticeable limp most of the day. He glared across the dark room at Jimmy Conklin, whose snaggle-toothed jaw was shiny purple and swollen.

"I can't believe you missed that old turd with the scatter-gun," he muttered, plenty loud for the boy to hear him.

Conklin, who was still holding the twelve gauge turned to face him, an insane look of hate in his bloody eyes. "You didn't do any better."

"I didn't have time to aim like you did," Carl whined. The kid was a punk, but he did have the shotgun, and Carl had unwisely left the rifle leaning by the doorway.

Pete held up a small, but thick hand. "Both of you shut up," he said shaking his head and staring at the thick braided rug. "He's gone. Killing him would have bought us some time, but we weren't planning on staying here forever anyway." He walked to the refrigerator with sure graceful movements of a leopard. Though he was sixteen years older than the oldest of the two men, neither questioned his authority. He had made one thing all too clear in prison; if Pete Miller said shut up, you shut up or faced grave consequences.

The light from the open generator-powered refrigerator silhouetted the compact outline of his powerful body, and, silently, both other men stared at him, waiting for his next command. "What we need now is something to eat." He took some elk steaks and threw them on the table. "Jimmy … Jim, it looks like there's a bowl of left over stew in here for you. Don't look like you'll be eating steak for a while."

The rich, heavy aroma of frying elk steaks soon filled the small cabin. Pete was able to find some of Rose's homemade bread and half a huckleberry pie. While he cooked, Jimmy and Carl looked through the rest of the cabin for clothes and other supplies and tried to keep their minds off the food. Conklin hurt too bad to think about it much, but

Carl was so hungry he would have eaten the steak raw and the smell of the cooking meat tantalized his exhausted body.

Clothes made for Harvey Sloan, a large man fit Carl perfectly, except for being tight in the belly. Carl brought out all the wool shirts in the old man's closet and three pair of blue jeans. Throwing his filthy prison blues into the corner, he changed into a heavy brown shirt and the largest pair of jeans. Both Miller and Conklin changed as well, making do by rolling up pant legs and sleeves.

The thick steaks were just getting warm inside when Pete slapped them on two plates and slid one across the table to Carl. He cut himself a healthy slice of bread and smeared it with butter. Conklin's stew was bubbling on the edge of the stove and he helped himself. It was difficult for him to eat with all the damage done to his mouth, but he found if he used just one side and chewed slowly he could almost enjoy his meal.

Fearing the law would be along any time, Miller shoved back away from the table with a resounding belch and got to his feet. Conlkin was not three quarters done with his stew and shoved the last few spoonfuls quickly into his mouth hitting the stub of his broken tooth in the process. He would have let loose a string of loud profanities but his mouth was full of hot stew so he made do with thinking them instead.

While Jimmy went out to catch the horses, Carl searched the bedroom for anything of value. He found no jewelry, Rose was not that kind of woman. A wedding band was all she would wear, shunning anything else as too gaudy. Under a tall, oak chest of drawers he did find a wooden chest with fifteen-hundred and twenty dollars inside. He was standing in the middle of the bedroom floor surrounded by a pile of clothes and holding the fat wad of money when Pete stepped through the door.

"Hope you were planing on sharing that with the rest of us," Pete said.

"Sure Pete. You at least." Carl glanced out the window at the light in the barn. "I don't see any reason to split with the puke though."

"Just split it three ways Carl," Pete said without a hint of emotion and turned toward the door. "And while you're snooping around in here look for a better map. All I found was a road map and I need a topo."

"I will." Carl carefully counted out three piles of money on the bed. He turned to make sure Pete was gone before softly cursing him under his breath. Even so, he put the extra twenty dollar bill in Pete's pile.

At ten-thirty PM, just over two and a half hours after Harvey Sloan had jumped the fence bareback and escaped into the woods, the three outlaws were packed and ready to move out. Jimmy had picked the three best looking horses. All had spent years on pack and dude strings and stood quietly for saddling. The stew had cooled his temper some and the six aspirin he took for dessert had reduced the pain in his head to a digging, knife like throb.

The skies finally decided to open up shortly after ten and the horses stood tied inside the cramped alleyway of the barn. Pete wore a brown slicker he found hanging inside the cabin door and the other two men made do with camouflage nylon ponchos the Sloans kept for their dudes. With blankets rolled up in pieces of canvas tarp tied behind their saddles, and as much food as they could stuff into their saddle bags, the three men untied their horses and climbed aboard.

Carl led his lazy eyed palomino over to a bale of straw so he would have a step to mount his horse.

"Won't be no steps all the time out there in the woods." said Conklin who was already in the saddle.

"I'll do alright." Carl sniffled a groan as he hauled himself onto the horse. He was sure the kid had purposely given him a tall one, but he wasn't about to give anyone the pleasure of hearing him complain. Riding loosely like a sack of potatoes, he trotted the horse from one end of the barn to the other. His elbows flapped like chicken wings and he had a tendency to cant to the left since he favored that knee.

Jimmy shook his head and sneered. "You'll be on the ground before we cross the first hill."

Pete hadn't been horseback since he was a teenager but he took to it and soon had his strawberry roan pointed north into the dark, wet woods ahead of him. He had no real plan as to how far they would go that night. He just wanted to put some miles between them and the cabin.

Just to confuse the trackers they opened the corral gate and chased the remaining horses and mules out into the darkness. Carl fired the Mini into the air to scatter them. Pete was fairly sure the animals would just come back to the pen but that would be after they had gone and he hoped the extra tracks would slow any lawmen looking for their trail.

He knew there would be cops at the cabin by morning. They would be chomping at the bit to get on the trail of someone who took down one of their own. He also knew it would take them a while to get organized. There were usually too many chiefs and not enough Indians from what he had seen. If they were like the ones Miller dealt with in the past, they probably wouldn't get their act together before noon. He chuckled at how inept cops were and allowed himself to relax a notch or two at the thought. Kicking his lanky roan up the trail, he shook his head in the darkness. No, there was no way anyone would be on their trail until well after noon.

CHAPTER EIGHT
Monday

It was ten minutes to five in the morning when Skip wheeled his Ford one-ton onto a wide gravel lot big enough to turn the whole rig around, four horse trailer and all. The drive up the sloppy, slick red clay of the mountain road had been a white knuckle affair and he was glad to see the flat. He and Terry had both been up for three hours loading horses and gear and although they were tired, adrenaline and the prospects of a good chase kept them awake.

The rain started shortly after ten the night before and showed no sign of a let up. Terry stared out the window at the downpour worrying about Christina. The call from the County about old man Sloan came in just after midnight. The baby had a touch of colic, and Christina was up with him when the phone rang. By the time Terry hung up, tears were streaming down her smooth, white cheeks.

She rocked back and forth in the wooden rocker beside their bed, wet drops falling onto the blonde hair of the sleeping baby at her breast. "We've got to go after them." Terry said patting her tiny hand. Christina was prone to bad dreams from time to time, and he supposed she'd had a bad one. They were usually about him not coming home.

She continued to rock, clutching the baby tightly, he woke up and joined her in her cry. "I know you do," she said. Wiping the tears from her eyes, she began to regain her composure. "And I know you can take care of yourself, I just can't help but worry."

"I'll be careful." he said, kissing her softly on the forehead. Even around Skip, Terry tried to keep his emotions in check. He had spent the better part of his life cultivating a stoicism and aloofness that helped him deal with problems in a detached, methodical manner. His martial arts training helped, but his spirit, the personality he was born with, was naturally quiet and distant. Christina hadn't tried to change him. Instead she nurtured the tender feelings she saw in him and fed that part of his personality. Consequentially, if he did let loose, it was around her.

"Look Chris," he whispered, kneeling beside her. "Everything is going to be alright, I promise."

"You'll have to look out for Skip. He seems in a rage."

"I will, and he'll look after me. That's what we always do."

She felt herself slipping again and just nodded, not wanting to disturb the baby anymore than she already had.

"What do you say we say a little prayer before I go?"

"I'd like that," she sniffed.

"Kiss the boys before you leave." she said when Terry finished with the prayer and was about to leave. The bedroom was dark and a shaft of light cut in from the hall, backlighting him.

He nodded. "I will. I love you," he whispered and blew her a kiss. She blew one back, and he ducked, catching it on the top of his smooth, bald head. It was their ritual goodbye.

"See you soon," she said, as he pulled the bedroom door shut and left her bathing in the sad green glow of the digital clock beside their lonely bed.

"This isn't going to make tracking these guys any easier," Terry said as much to himself as Skip. He was not the least bit worried about his own prospects at catching Wally's killers, but his wife's mood had made him melancholy.

Skip nodded, setting the parking brake and killing the rattling diesel engine. He was happy to be about the business of chasing the bad guys and felt optimistic for the first time in two days. "Not at first anyway, but once we strike their trail, there ought to be plenty of sign. If they took some of Sloan's horses, which I'm sure they did, there will be plenty of tracks in all this muck."

"True enough. But first we have to cross their trail."

"Are you kidding? With an intrepid tracker such as yourself, that should be no trouble at all. You forget, I've seen you find a drop of elk blood the size of a dog tick, ten minutes after it was too dark for me to see my own boots." Skip opened a brown paper sack on the seat between them and pitched a sausage biscuit to his friend. "Let's just sit here a minute and see if this rain'll let up. It's too dark to track yet anyway."

Skip was just biting into his biscuit when Sheriff Earl Nelson came slogging up to the truck window. He wore a yellow slicker and a plastic cover over his brown uniform Stetson. Though in most ways a buffoon himself, Sheriff Nelson was smart enough to surround himself with capable people. So far, that had been enough to keep him in office. He

was a small, skeletal man with a wad of tobacco that seemed bigger than his tiny head sticking out above a bony jaw. A constant trickle of the greasy, brown stuff drooled from the corners of his mouth when he thought the voting public was not around, but the minute the papers or his wife showed up, he became starched shirts and breath mints; the picture of public office.

Rain dripping off the brim of his hat, the sheriff rapped on the driver's side door. Skip cracked the window and told him to get in the back seat. Grateful for pickups with four doors, Nelson clamored in behind the two marshals and next to a frowning blue heeler. The warm, peppery smell of sausage biscuits filled the cab of the truck and Nelson noticed the heeler had one of her own on the seat between her paws. She eyed him warily, and he decided to let her keep it.

"If it isn't the High Sheriff of Sanders County Montana," said Skip over his shoulder. "What can we do for you Sheriff?"

"I thought this rain was supposed to stop by daybreak," he said taking off his dripping hat and keeping an eye on the dog.

"It's not daybreak yet." Terry still looked out the window into the darkness. He had no use for Nelson or any other politician, for that matter.

"Well it'll be light soon and I don't expect this is going to let up from the looks of things. Where are the state boys, I wonder. This is their deal isn't it?"

"They're pretty busy working the roads," said Skip. "I'm sure they'll be along shortly."

"What's the plan as far as you fellows know? I got two deputies and some horses over there."

Skip adjusted the stampede string on his high crowned silver belly hat. It was much too nice a hat to wear out in the rain. His father gave it to him when he was eighteen as a Sunday hat, but Skip turned it into a using hat when he moved to Montana. He called it his 'lucky lid' and he wore it only when he felt he was on an important job.

"We figured on waiting 'til light so's not to mess up any tracks that might be left," Skip said, putting the hat on his head and his hand on the door handle. "By then, the state boys'll be here and you all can do a crime scene. Everybody agrees our bandits are probably headed toward Canada so we'll just search around that direction until we cut their trail. Does that suit you Sheriff?"

Nelson nodded, relieved someone else had made a plan before he was forced to himself.

By five-forty, muted shadows became visible in the soggy morning air. Because of the mountains to the east, the Sloan place didn't see the sun until eight, even on a clear day. The rain slowed to an occasional drop, but the sky still boiled, heavy and foreboding above their heads. It was going to be a dark morning.

Terry busied himself with laying out the gear on the back of the pickup. Even with the pack mule, they'd travel light. Each man packed a canvas bedroll on his own saddle horse. In addition to that, each carried a pair of binoculars, jerky, and a canteen. Terry brought his scoped 300 Winchester Magnum. He rarely left home without it. The gun was outside Marshals Service regulations, by a long way, but had a far greater reach than his pistol, and he felt more comfortable with it nearby when he was in the mountains. Wally named it 'Elkslayer' the year before when Terry killed his tenth bull.

The mule hauled food for the two men, as well as extra grain for the animals. There was probably still good grass in the mountains, but Skip reasoned they should keep their horses in top shape during the ride. Had it been any other mule but Fish, they would have done without a pack animal.

Terry looked off toward Trestle Creek where Skip had taken the stock to water. Fish, true to his name had waded out into the middle of the rain swollen stream. The stocky mule always stayed married to his buttermilk mare. He never strayed far from her side and just followed along behind her on the trail. For this reason, Skip never tied him. He was an easy keeper with a personality to match, which allowed the two marshals to keep their minds on matters at hand. Belle lay on the bank, watchful as ever over her man, conserving her energy for whatever lay ahead.

They decided to plan on a five day trip and had provisioned enough food. If things took longer, they could make it eight by rationing. In addition to food, the mule also packed an axe, a single burner gas stove, a small nylon tent, and three sets of handcuffs and leg irons. Both men wore oilskin slickers and each carried an extra heavy wool sweater in his bedroll. Even if the weather turned off cold at night they would be ready.

Terry adjusted the Glock .40 on his belt and checked to make sure both spare magazines were in place. With the gun and both reloads, he had nearly a box of ammo at his finger tips. The rain slowed to a drizzle and Terry, always hot blooded, threw his slicker over the back of the tailgate to enjoy the morning air. In a dark, brown canvas shirt with his jeans tucked into the tall shafts of heavy leather boots, the only thing that kept him from looking like a page out of a history book was the ugly, black pistol on his side. It didn't match the rest of his outfit, but if any one noticed they didn't comment. A black flat brimmed hat hung by a horse hair stampede string against his shoulder blades. His bald head and drooping mustache, combined with his natural swagger, gave him the air of a gunfighter come to do some serious business. Ugly black gun or not, Terry McGreggor looked, and was, a force to be reckoned.

Skip led the two horses up the gentle slope from the creek to the trailer, talking to them softly out of habit. Fish followed dutifully, munching a piece of watercress he'd plucked from the bottom of the stream like a moose. Terry took the mare's lead rope, and Skip led Jake to the other side of the truck, where his high canteled saddle sat across the bed rail. Fish, realizing the horses were being tied for a while, munched on a stand of wild timothy near the edge of the gravel pad.

Wanting to get on the trail as quickly as possible, the men tacked up their mounts without speaking. Both horses had been hayed well on the trip and stood quietly once they were saddled.

After finishing with Jake, Skip caught Fish by the halter. Attaching a cotton lead rope, he tied the mule to the trailer beside the dun mare. He and Terry had packed enough times together each knew his task and they had the mule's Decker on and loaded in ten minutes.

Checking the quick release 'bank robbers' knot on the mules lead rope, Skip rubbed his long ears. "Now Fish, I aim to leave you tied for a few minutes while we look for some tracks. That is, if you won't throw too much of a fit being away from your girlfriend for a minute or two."

Terry checked his cinch one last time and swung into the saddle. "You think he'll go nuts without her?"

"Wouldn't you?" Skip said petting the dun on her broad, round rump. "I mean, just look at her. She's beautiful."

Terry shook his head and urged his horse toward the corral. "Come on. It's getting light enough to see tracks."

Fish brayed once when they walked away and then resigned himself to a few minutes of loneliness with a long heavy sigh.

Two county deputies and Sheriff Nelson trotted up to meet them outside the wood rail fence at Sloan's. Two state investigators had arrived from Helena, and they stood at the open gate studying the ground. Both men looked to be in their late forties and could have been brothers. Each was tall, over six feet, and had dark hair, greyed at the temples. They weren't part of the uniformed service but each wore tan twill slacks and a rust colored Gor-Tex rain coat.

"Looks like Mutt and Jeff," Skip said when he saw them.

"More like Mutt and Mutt," Terry said with a quiet chuckle. "Twins."

Skip tipped his hat back and crossed his hands on the saddle horn in thought. "Or Jeff and Jeff. I can't ever remember which one was tallest."

The two state investigators seemed affable enough though, and stuck to their job of investigating the crime scene with the sheriff. Skip doubted either of them had ever been on a horse. Not that that made them lesser men … not much anyway.

Rain had obscured most of the tracks and the remaining ones were full of water. Once at the corral, the men were able to see two more horses at the edge of the tree-line grazing on the rich meadow grass. "Looks like they let the rest of the horses out," said the tall deputy with a thin mustache and a Montana crease on his brown uniform hat.

Terry eyed the ground from the back of his horse. "Just look for tracks of horses that are carrying people then."

Nelson snorted and spit a slick slurry of brown juice on the wet ground. "Right!"

"I think he's serious, boss," said the other deputy; a young baby-faced man who shaved once a week, whether he needed to or not.

"How many horses did the old man have?" asked Dawson, one of the State men.

"Eleven," said the baby-faced County deputy. "Counting the Appaloosa he rode out on."

"That leaves seven animals loose if our bandits only took three," Skip said, twisting in the saddle to get a 360° view of the area. "I imagine most of them are close." He looked down at the sheriff. "I wonder if you could have one of your men help me look in the barn for some oats to throw to the loose stock. That will get them out of our way."

The sheriff nodded at the tall deputy, who, after tying his own horse to the top rail, slogged off toward the barn with Skip .

"Is that the one he calls the dun mare?" Nelson gestured at the horse Terry was riding.

Terry nodded.

The sheriff spit a thick stream of brown juice into the mud. "How come he never gave her a name? His gelding has a name, his mare should have a name."

Terry chuckled and shook his head. "She's got a name. It's top secret though, so he never uses it." Without another word, Terry wheeled the mare and pointed her toward the woods.

When the hissing sound of oats dumped into the feed bunk filtered through the foggy air, fir and tamaracks surrounding the woods came alive with horses and mules. Two that were grazing in plain sight were the first in the corral and the others followed in a matter of minutes, the blue heeler happily yipping at their heels and working them the direction they were going anyway.

Terry watched with interest as the animals materialized from the dark, drifting, mist of the forest. None of them could have been more than a few yards away, but only the two out grazing had been visible. Terry

knew how easy it was to hide in the thick mountain forests. He'd followed many an elk into a tangled thicket only to have it vanish without
a trace. As a small boy his grandfather told him the big bulls could fold
their antlers up behind them so they could move through thick brush
and downed lodgepole pines. He never quite believed the story. He
knew the woods didn't swallow things. Everything went somewhere, it
was just a matter of thinking like whatever you were tracking. If you
knew what an elk did when it was pushed, it didn't matter if it folded
up it's rack and put it in a suitcase, it couldn't get away without a trace.
Now he had to think like an outlaw who was running for his life.

Keeping his eyes glued to the ground, Terry began to work his way
back and forth, in and out of the trees. There were game trails every
where, and the large cloven prints of elk that came to steal hay from
the Sloans plowed the soggy ground.

Skip squeezed Jake into a easy lope and headed north of the barn
about three hundred yards up an open drainage. His hands were quiet,
and he rode with his legs. The bay was used to his ways and moved according to the shifts of his body. They'd worked together enough that
anyone watching thought the horse could read Skips mind. Most times,
Skip agreed.

Working his way back along the edge of the tree line, he dropped
the soft rope rein and slowed the horse by leaning back slightly in the
saddle. Jake dropped back into a walk immediately, the smooth, rawhide
hackamore around his roman nose, never coming into play.

The mountain above the Sloan cabin, slanting gradually up from the
valley floor, was a rough tangle of Douglas fir, shrubby wild raspberry,
and devils claw. Dark green leaves of mountain alder dripped rainwater
on the smaller, perfumed foliage of late huckleberry bushes.

Terry worked toward Skip, having no luck in the trees to the northeast.
A game trail turned small stream, crossed directly in front of him and
led up the side of the mountain disappearing into a stand of scraggly
hemlock forty yards away. Rivulets of dirty, brown water washed down
the narrow pathway, worn into the side of the hill from years of elk and
deer travel. The water moved fast enough to cover and erase any tracks
that might have been there even a moment before. Stepping the mare
through a muddy pool at the base of the trail, Terry started to ride on,
but something a few feet up the side of the incline caused him to stop.
Without knowing exactly what he had seen, he whistled Skip over and
jumped off his horse into the mud.

The game trail started at the edge of what was actually an old logging road and headed strait up the side of the mountain for about six feet before angling off toward the hemlocks.

Just at the point where the trail cut back along the side hill, there was a gouge in the dirt on the uphill edge of the trail.

Terry grasped a handful of dripping buck brush and pulled himself up the slippery slope. When he got to the divot in the mud, he smiled and whistled under his breath.

"Got you now," he whispered.

Skip trotted up on Jake. In the saddle, he was almost eye level with Terry as he squatted on the game trail. "Whatcha find?"

Instead of speaking, Terry moved to one side and pointed.

Although the rain had covered the horse tracks in the trail, pushed into the muddy side hill was a perfect impression of a stirrup bottom and the toe of a boot.

"The horse must have slipped here," Terry pointed to where the trail cut back. "When he went down, one of our boys caught a foot on the side there."

Skip eyed the hemlock grove up the mountain. "You Deputy Mc-Greggor, are one hawk-eyed law-dawg."

Once they knew where to look, there was sign every where. Halfway between the trees and the first stirrup print, the trail leveled off considerably and tracks off three shod horses were clearly visible in the muck.

Terry looked at his watch. It was just after eight AM.

Skip and Terry were getting the mule when a green Forest Service Jeep Cherokee came slithering up the mountain and squished to a halt on the gravel pad beside the other vehicles. Skip shook his head when he saw Lieutenant Forbisher climb out wearing a bright yellow slicker. The tubby man made his way to the corral, where the county deputies stood beside their horses. He chose his steps carefully, as if he intended to cross two hundred feet of slick, black mud without wrecking the polish on his boots.

"Hello Sheriff," Forbisher smiled stiffly. He nodded at the two Sanders County deputies and looked at Skip and Terry who trotted up with the mule. "Marshals," he said tipping his head.

Belle looked at him from her spot beside Jake's foreleg and growled. She was an excellent judge of character.

"You've found their trail then?" The Lieutenant asked, finding himself a relatively dry rock to perch on.

"That we have L.T.," said Terry.

"Care to join us?" Skip asked, knowing full well there was no danger in that happening.

Forbisher shook his head. "No, they still have to cross several roads, and I'd rather be in front of them than behind them. This way, we know which way they are going. I don't mind you two following; I appreciate it. The pressure may cause them to get sloppy and ride right into our road blocks."

"Maybe," Terry said. He started to say more but decided against it. Things were working out better than he expected. He was more than happy to let Forbisher keep his faith in patrol cars while he and Skip went about sacking up the outlaws and bringing them to justice.

The Lieutenant reached under his raincoat and took out a black plastic box the size of a thick wallet. He held it up to Skip. "You can reach us on this cell phone from most of the higher mountains around here. I want you to keep us abreast of any sighting and so on."

Skip took the phone and stuck it in his pommel bag. He doubted it would work, but like Terry, wanted to be shed of Forbisher and get on the trail. Knowing the outlaws had at least a six hour head start, both men were anxious to close the gap.

Terry lead the procession, with Skip behind him and Fish strolling along in the rear at an easy rolling walk. Belle worked the ground in between, using her stored energy to dart this way and that along the trail. She paused every so often to sniff at a peculiar track or twig and scurried back to the departing troop.

Skip patted the leather pouch hanging across the front of his saddle-horn, then turned to Forbisher and the other lawmen as he wheeled Jake up the trail. "We'll call when we get a chance," he yelled over his shoulder. He urged the horse into a trot to keep up with Terry. "And if we can't call ... we'll write."

The deputies nodded and the taller one took of his hat. "Run them into the roadblocks boys," he yelled, watching them work their way up the side-hill where the tracks began. It was apparent from the pained look on his face he wished he was riding off after outlaws with the two marshals. "Or bring 'em back yourselves," he said under his breath. Looking at Forbisher, he knew that would more than likely be the case.

CHAPTER NINE

The tracks were easy to follow up the side of the mountain where the rain was running off, leaving them visible to even an untrained eye. Once they crossed the ridge line, the tracks meandered off the trail around some deadfall and along a wide slope of talus shale. If the horses hadn't been shod, it might have been harder to track them. As it was, even on the wet, grey rock, the metal shoes left tell tale scuffs and scratches.

The two lawmen adopted the same routine they used to track a wounded elk. Terry, by far the better tracker, kept his eyes on the ground, letting them play along the mud and grass as his horse plodded slowly along. He had a sixth sense when it came to following a trail and even when he lost it, he could usually snoop it out again.

But they weren't tracking elk—more like wounded grizzly. So, while Terry kept his eye floating up and down the trail, Skip surveyed the country, watchful for a shadow or reflection off metal. Likely, the outlaws knew they were being followed, and one, or all, of them could circle back at any time to check their back trail.

Skip found it difficult to be much of a lookout. The blowing feathers of heavy fog and the drizzle made it impossible to see more than a few yards. Sounds were muffled by the wet, but the two kept their conversations low and hushed.

The smells of the mountains were all around them in the damp. Skip grabbed a handful of grand fir needles as he rode and crushed them between his fingers. The flat, green needles smelled like spiced orange tea and reminded him of Christmas. Ozone drifted up from the moist, decaying, forest floor, giving the air a rich, clean aroma. He alternately thought about Kate and Wally, letting his mind float back and forth, from warmth to melancholy.

Terry kept his mind on the trail. He had been a Ranger sniper in the military, and combined with his martial arts training, this gave him plenty of focusing practice. At times, when the trail was obvious and easy, he stole a moment to think of his sons and the way Christina cried before he left. He knew these men were killers and nothing to be trifled with, but he considered himself no trifle of a man, either. Terry supposed his confidence is what scared Christina. Maybe she felt he was over confident. Maybe he was.

By noon, he estimated they had gone ten miles, not including the wide circles they made trying to pick up the trail in a beaver bog choked with broad leafed skunk cabbage. They wasted a half hour on that, but true to his reputation, Terry struck the trail where the three outlaws had almost doubled back on themselves. It was obvious they knew they were being followed.

The morning turned out to be an ambling, up and down affair. Since Miller and his tiny band had no idea where they were going, they seldom took the most direct route. Twice, tracks disappeared into dense lodge-pole snags that should have stopped a rabbit, only to spill out again on the other side.

In a narrow, alder-choked valley once serving as a logging road, Skip dismounted to check Fish's pack and give Jake a breather before starting up the steep ridge ahead. Terry squatted over the trail holding his mare by the reins and looking at the jumble of tracks in the muddy bottom. The rain had let up but the clouds, low and angry, hovered just above their heads.

"They got down here to rest too," Terry said. "Looks like one of them is keeping apart from the other two." Terry pointed to a set of tracks off to the side of the main trail, well away from the others.

Skip walked over, leading Jake on a loose reign. "Miller?" He hunkered down to study the footprints. They had seen nothing but horse tracks all morning, and it was satisfying to know for certain that bodies were riding the animals they followed.

"I imagine. From the files, I'd figure him to be the leader. Looks like they stopped here to stretch their legs. One of them had to use a stump over there to remount."

Skip snorted, the corners of his mouth turning up in an evil grin. "I hope it's the one who lost the teeth."

He looked at the mountain that lay ahead of them. It was tall and sinister, with only a tall spruce or tamarack stuck up here and there to pierce a dark, misty shroud. The trail, disappearing into the mist, was strewn with flat grey rocks obviously fallen from somewhere above. No tracks came back down from the fog, so the killers had gone that way despite the danger of avalanche and rock slide.

"They're dang lucky they stole the right type of horses," Skip observed still staring up into the black clouds. "Flatland horses would be laying dead in a pile, right here at the bottom of this hill. These guys are going to make a mistake soon or have an accident. This country's just too rough, and they don't know any better than to take the roughest route."

Terry still studied Miller's track. "He might not know the country but I think he knows there are easier routes. It's a lot easier to crash through the brush when you're being chased than when you're doing the chasing. I figure he's thinking if he takes the hard road, we might get tripped up as easily as he does."

"True," Skip agreed. He remembered being a green rookie at Ft. Worth when his training officer got into a pursuit of some guys who robbed a Seven Eleven. They were going over eighty when the robbers took the Interstate going the wrong way. Those outlaws had no way of knowing Skip's training officer was a Nascar driver on his off time and a few cars coming his direction didn't discourage him in the least.

"I wonder if he knows we're friends of the trooper he killed," Skip said, not really expecting an answer.

Terry put his hand across the boot print left by Miller and felt the cool, wet earth. Sometimes, it seemed a track left more behind than just an impression in the mud. He found himself wondering if these men would let themselves be brought in. They had killed at least one man. Each faced the death penalty and Terry knew either he or Skip could easily carry out the sentence themselves. People half expected it. Terry was a hard man, but he was no killer, if he didn't have to be. No matter how much he talked about it, neither was Skip.

Belle was busy zigzagging back and forth across the flat, investigating each clump of grass and footprint. She stopped, growling at the spot where one of the killers had relieved himself in the bushes.

"I guess she's got their scent now, although I've never seen a pup quite like that before." The voice came from behind the two lawmen and startled both of them. They drew their pistols in the blink of an eye. As much as he loved Jake, Skip instantly ducked behind him and used the horse as a shield between him and the stranger. Terry had nowhere to hide but his pistol whooshed out of his leather holster at the first sound behind him and he took up all the slack in the trigger, ready to fire.

Neither the dog or the horses heard the old man come up, but when he spoke Belle cocked her head in his direction and trotted over to him as if he were an old friend. The man had long snow white hair, worn in two braids tied with pieces of dark leather and a flowing white beard. Dressed in brown wool pants and grey sweater of the same material. He raised his hands high above his head and a broad smile spread across his thinish lips.

"Hold on boys," he said, his steel-grey eyes flickering, as if it were a sunny day instead of drizzling rain. "I'm here to help."

Skip kept his gun trained on the man and stepped from behind Jake. He had seen photos of the escapees and the man matched none of them. "Help us do what?"

Terry who had stayed in a squat when he drew his gun stood up and looked at the old man. It was hard to figure his age. He could have been fifty, or eighty. He seemed fit enough though. Old, but not the least bit frail. Terry slowly realized he had seen the man before; sitting on the fence at the firing range.

Letting his hands fall to his sides, the old man wearily shook his head. "To help you catch those desperados of course. It makes me sad you men don't recognize me; a couple of good Danite's such as yourselves."

Terry dropped the mare's reins and rubbed his eyes. Both men holstered their guns, for in an instant, they had no doubt who stood before them. The man reached down and scratched Belle behind the ears. She gave him a wide toothy grin and groaned with pleasure.

"Yes ma'am, you know who I am, don't you girl? You'd think these two infant lawdawgs could recognize Orrin Porter Rockwell."

CHAPTER 10

Jimmy Conklin's nerves were raw as hamburger. He was by far the best horseman of the three; and that was a mercy, for if he bounced around as much as Carl, he felt sure his head would have fallen right off his shoulders. Miller was in the lead, scouting far up the trail and trying to figure a way to stump whoever might be tracking them. By now, all of them had sense enough to know they were being followed. It was plain, bad luck old Sloan had gotten away. If things had gone according to plan, they might have made it clear to Canada before anyone knew where they were headed.

As it turned out, they had ridden all night and were still riding. The only enjoyment Jimmy got besides being out of prison was watching Carl try and stay on his bouncing horse; and that was much less funny as the day wore on. They had been in the saddle over twenty hours and he needed to get down and rest his head. Conklin didn't doubt Miller would kill him if he bucked his authority, but that meant catching him first.

Jimmy spent what time he wasn't in juvenile hall, poaching with his drunk uncle and knew the mountains better than either of the other two men. That's why they wanted him along, and why they wouldn't let him leave. His head was getting worse though, and he felt if he did not get some rest soon, he'd be of no use at all. He knew they'd kill him then. As the day wore on, he watched the others and figured out different ways to slip away. Of course, he still had the shotgun. He thought about killing them both, but the incident with Sloan shook his confidence. He was certain if he shot the big gun, his head would explode along with the shell. Besides, he didn't know how close the cops were and didn't want them zeroing in on any shots, if he did survive.

They had crossed several forest service roads and Jimmy was pretty sure he had seen this area before. If he was correct, there was a fair sized ranch house not too far to the northeast. That would be a good place to rest, and the others wouldn't know about it. His head throbbed so badly his thoughts became fuzzy. He needed to get away while he still could. Jimmy knew he could out run Meeks even with a splitting head. The fool wouldn't be able to stay in the saddle long enough to chase him. He was glad Miller didn't have the rifle. It would be harder to get a decent shot with a pistol. He hoped the others would feel the same as he did and not want to risk firing a shot.

Checking his horse, Jimmy let Carl get a little farther ahead. The fat man listed heavily to his left, half asleep in the saddle as his horse started a long steady climb toward Pete, who was almost a hundred yards up the trail looking for a way around a huge tangle of deadfall timber. To the right of the trail, twenty feet down the steep embankment, an old skid trail was visible through the alder brush. If Pete was closer, he might have tried it, but Meeks would never risk trying the loose gravel over the steep edge.

Jimmy looked through a bloody red haze at his escape route. He tried to set his teeth in determination, but winced at the pain. He knew if he thought too long, he might talk himself out of the plan. Getting away would be painful. His horse had a stiff trot and he was sure the gallop wouldn't be much better. Gathering the reins in his left hand, he held the shot gun out in front with his right hand to protect his swollen face from the net of tangled alder branches and dug his heels into the geldings ribs, forcing him over the slippery bank. The horse locked up both front legs, and squatting low on his haunches, slid down the loose mud and gravel. Loose shale skittered down behind them and the horse hit the bottom with a bone jarring thump. Not happy about leaving the herd, the animal whirled and floundering against the bank, tried to climb back up the sloppy incline.

Jimmy's head spun as the horse jarred him. Things around him grew darker and his stomach lurched into his throat. He was breathing hard from the excitement of his escape, and the cold air drawing across the exposed nerves of his teeth was excruciating. He swayed in the saddle, thinking for a moment he would pass out, but his anger at the unwilling horse yanked him back into consciousness. Striking brutally with the shotgun butt, he gave the gelding a sharp crack to the side of the head.

The big animal was stunned for an instant and dropped back off the embankment, this time keeping to the lower trail.

The rattle of sliding rock and stiff whack of the shotgun hitting horse hide, pulled Carl out of his riding stupor. He turned just in time to watch the kid and his horse disappear into the tangled thatch of the skid trail.

Jimmy wasted no time looking back, but kicked his horse into full gallop as quick as he was pointed in the right direction. The jarring impact and jigging horse had hurt to the quick, but now the rocking gallop of his get away was smooth relief. Elk often used the same skid road and while it was grown up in huckleberry and bitterbrush, there was a distinguishable trail. Jimmy found it fairly easy to keep his horse at a decent, almost bearable, ground-eating gallop.

He had no idea if he was being followed but decided it best not to play his whole hand just in case. He stayed to what he thought was a parallel route to the ranch. When he was sure the other two had given up, it would be an easy matter to cut over and find him a warm dry place to lie down and rest.

He desperately needed more medicine for his head. It seemed the pounding behind his ear had lessened some just by being rid of Pete and Carl. Apart from his broken teeth, maybe there wasn't anything a long soak in a hot bath and sleep in a real bed wouldn't set to right. If he remembered, there were a couple of teenage sisters at the ranch as well.

Jimmy slowed his horse to a gentle, rocking-horse lope and looked down at the shotgun in his right hand. As bad as it would hurt his head to use it, if anyone at the ranch tried to come between him and his plans, he would surely make them sorry.

Back on the trail, Miller turned at the sound of Carl's whistle and trotted his tired roan back down the hill.

"Where'd Jimmy go?" Miller said, a deadly look in his eye.

"Couldn't tell you Pete," said Carl trying to stay cavalier. Miller's gaze terrified him, and he squirmed in the saddle despite himself . "I was just riding along and suddenly he bailed off the edge of the trail."

Miller said nothing and gave no quarter from the terrible stare. Sitting on his tall red horse, with swirling mist turning his dark brown slicker black, the man looked like the devil himself. Even Carl's cross-eyed palomino began to feel uncomfortable and pawed at the soggy ground.

Seething inside at his own incompetence for escaping with a cripple and a kid with too much of a mind of his own, Miller spat on the ground. The fact that Jimmy split off could actually slow down, or split up, whatever law was after them. Miller's biggest problem was that he didn't trust the kid if he got caught, to spill his guts about where they were going. He didn't know much, but he knew a little, and a little was enough to ruin a good plan.

Instead of yelling at Carl or running after the deserter, the old outlaw took a long, slow breath, and shook his head. Even when he wheeled and trotted away, his lanky horse splashing in the drizzle, Carl found he couldn't relax. Miller hadn't blown, but that didn't mean he wasn't primed and lit.

Carl had seen the same behavior before. Once, a Mexican had checked out a particular book Pete wanted from the prison library. Pete told him he wanted the book but the man refused to give it up. When no immediate fight broke out, the young Mexican unwisely relaxed. He was found dead in the shower a week later, a sharpened toothbrush in his kidney. Peter Miller never forgot somebody he didn't like.

Looking over his shoulder at the direction Jimmy disappeared, Carl sighed a tired sigh. At least in prison when his leg hurt he could rest. It ached badly from the uneven gait of the stiff legged horse. He felt sure the kid gave him a rough walking horse on purpose. Besides its stiff gate, the horse was a palomino—a blonde. Carl's ex-wife was a blonde. She had been hard to get along with too, and now that he thought back on it, a little cross eyed. He cursed Jimmy Conklin for picking him a horse that was so much like Helen.

Now the kid had run away, and there was nobody but him for Pete to be mad at. For an instant, Meeks thought about running off himself. He looked back up the trail at Miller, who was beginning to disappear in the deepening fog. If he ran, he was sure he would fall off his horse—then Pete would ride up and shoot him. If he followed, Pete was likely to lose his temper and shoot him anyway. "Get shot now or get shot later," he mumbled his prospects to himself.

Never one to make a quick decision, Carl kicked the droop-eyed palomino with his sore leg and started up the trail after Miller. The rain picked up in intensity and dripped from the corners of his bushy black eyebrows. "Later is as good a time as any," he said to the wind.

CHAPTER 11

Neither Skip or Terry knew quite how to react. For several seconds both did nothing but stand and stare. Porter merely smiled a polite, if disarming smile and continued to scratch Belle behind the ears. Terry felt as if the wind had been knocked out of him, and Skip's mouth hung open.

It was Terry who first regained his composure. "You ... you ... really are ... Porter Rockwell." He whispered.

Rockwell stood and tipped his black, felt hat. "In the ... funny, I almost said, 'in the flesh,' but I guess that ain't exactly right."

Terry then did something Skip had never seen him do for any other man; he took off his hat. "It's an honor to meet you," he said. Skip took off his own hat but only managed a nod.

"Shoot boys, no honor in meeting me, I assure you. Fact is, I was getting a bit antsy on the other side. I found me a thin spot in the veil and seen you two might need some help, so I volunteered for the job."

Jake was starting to graze away from Skip and the reins slipping through his fingers snapped him out of his stupor. "You came back to help us hunt outlaws?" He pulled the horse closer for moral support.

"Hell ... I mean, heck no," Porter shot a skyward glance and grimaced. "I promised 'em I'd watch my language," he said quietly. When he seemed sure nothing was going to happen because of his cussing, he relaxed. "You boys are doin' a fine job of tracking. It's you that worries me. You're letting these desperados get to you and it's likely to get you done in before your appointed time." Porter drew a deep breath and looked around. "It's wonderful up there boys. Don't get me wrong. But, some men were made to be in pursuit. I envy you."

Skip put his hat back on. His head was getting wet and he felt a chill. "What does a man like you do, a … up there?" He heard himself ask.

"Oh there's plenty to do. I reckon I missed dealing with banditos too much to settle in well. It ain't exactly like they're hiring guards for the spirit prison, ya know."

Terry wiped his bald head with a bandanna and replaced his own hat. "So, you came to help us do what, then?"

"Your friend, Brother Fuller, asked me to look in on you and see that you're alright."

Skip took a step forward at the sound of his friend's name. "You've spoken with Wally?"

"Only for a minute. He's pretty busy. Fitting in nicely too, but he's worried about you, and his family." Porter kicked at the ground. "Seems he left in sort of a hurry."

"It's funny," Skip said, relaxing more with each word. "I've been so busy thinking about Wally, I never considered he might be thinking about me."

"You said he's worried about us." Terry was frowning. "Are we headed for a trap or something?"

"He ain't worried about you physically. He's worried about your spirits. Brother Fuller fears you're becoming unsettled, and that's no good way for a lawman. Take it from me." Porter slapped his hands together and smiled through his curly white beard. "I can't really explain it all in one breath. You have to warm up to this sort a thing." His cool grey eyes twinkled at the prospect of a new adventure. "Besides, I wouldn't mind riding along with you boys while we talk. Your pal did ask me to look out for you, and I ain't in a real big hurry to get back."

"Ride along?" Skip looked around for a horse.

Porter smiled and gestured over his shoulder toward a dense thicket of aspens, their leaves shimmering like silver dollars in the wet mountain air. "I left my horse tied back there. An old and unnecessary habit I reckon, but I figured it'd be easier on ya if I came in on foot. Too many spiritual manifestations at once can weaken a body."

While the old man went to fetch his mount, the two deputies could do little more than stand and stare at one another. Skip was the first to crack a smile.

"Terry are you seeing what I'm seeing?" He asked, rubbing his eyes and looking into the white-barked trees where Porter Rockwell disappeared.

"I'm 'fraid so partner." Terry said, finding the strength to climb into the saddle. His legs had suddenly become noodley when Porter appeared, and he had no intention of embarrassing himself in front of his hero.

"I've always wanted to meet the man, and I feel comfortable with the idea he's a g- ... I think we should keep this between us."

Skip swung a leg over his saddle. "You're reading my mind on that one."

A moment later Porter cleared the aspens on a massive black stallion with three white stockings and fiery eyes. The other horses noticed it, but paid little attention when Porter sidled up next to the mounted deputies and drew rein. The big black responded instantly and stopped, his crested neck and dark, flowing mane forming a graceful arch.

Skip patted Jake on the shoulder. "No offense boy, but if I could build a horse from scratch, that's the way I'd do it."

Terry looked the animal over. He was not the horse enthusiast Skip was, but he knew a remarkable animal when he saw one. Even in the drizzle, the stallion's coat shown like fine mink. "Impressive animal."

Porter Rockwell hunched forward in the saddle and winked. "I realize paradise ain't heaven, but it wouldn't be paradise either if they didn't have a horse a two. I was mighty glad to come across this one." Porter rubbed the animals broad neck and gave a satisfied nod. "Yes sir, it's amazing how well a horse'll cooperate when he understands what you're trying to say." He cocked his head toward Skip, recognizing him as a fellow horseman. "They don't get no smarter, mind ya. A few of the barriers just come down."

The three rode into the afternoon. The first mountain seemed imposing in the mist and fog, but Porter talked as they road, and time and distance melted together like the twinkling of an eye.

Terry read many times how Porter Rockwell could track better than any Indian. Until now, he had been more comfortable with his own skills, relying on intuition and training. Although he didn't brag about it, he felt himself a naturally good tracker. But now, in the shadow of a man who's name brought a hush of reverence to his voice, he felt inept. He tried to concentrate on the job at hand, but the fact that Porter was watching his every move flat unnerved him.

Porter must have sensed the man's predicament. "Where'd you learn to track? I'd say you was part Indian if ya had a top knot." The old man ran a hand through his snow white beard.

Terry looked up from the sloppy ground, trying to keep from grinning at such a compliment. "The military ... and hunting."

"Hunting men is an art ain't it?" Porter mused, bending forward in the saddle. His blue-grey eyes glistened with a thousand memories of manhunts and gun battles.

Skip found himself wondering how many stories of Rockwell and his exploits were true. Like Terry, he was taken with boyish fascination and for a moment thought about asking Porter about the stories. Then he remembered barrel-chested young Brother Grant asking Terry about killing people, and thought better. As it was, Porter seemed happy enough to entertain the men with stories. Some were familiar to them, some were not.

Terry led them around the base of a small hill. Tracks led up, but he saw no reason to climb it just to come down again. He recognized the country now, and it made his tracking job easier knowing where the creeks were and what lay on the other side of the mountains.

The trail widened out considerably in the flat at the bottom below the misty hill and Porter urged his horse up next to Skip. "Tell me about yourselves, I've been rambling on like a silly school girl."

The path around the base of the hill was straightforward and easy to follow for the moment, so Terry reined in his mare and let the others catch him.

Skip shrugged at the suggestion to talk about himself. "I suppose you know more about me than I could tell you."

Port smiled and shook his head. He looked like a concrete apparition, but a ghostly apparition in the light drizzle and swirling mist. Evening drew nearer. "I ain't a heavenly spy." He defended. "I know you had some troubles with this thing here, and your buddy was able to fill me in some, but that's not much. Have you got a woman for instance? How about young 'uns?"

Terry looked at Skip and answered first. "Married with four boys," he said. "I'm as happy as can be in that respect."

Porter turned his cool grey eyes toward Skip. "How about you Brother Garret?" The old man smiled eagerly and leaned forward in his saddle.

"I suppose I've had less than good luck with the female side of things." He went on to relate what happened with Brenda, leaving out most of the details. He was sure Porter had been through much the same.

"It's not all sorrow and sob though," Terry said, with an uncharacteristic gush of words. "You didn't mention Kate Beebe."

Rockwell raised a wary eyebrow. "Kate who? I'm not sure I heard you right."

"Beebe" Skip said, shooting a glance at Terry. He didn't like to talk about Kate, feeling that as long as he kept her to himself, she'd stay around and not evaporate like Brenda did.

Porter's normally smooth, high forehead wrinkled into a half scowl. "Is it serious with this Beebe girl?"

"I suppose you could say that." Skip nodded, resigned to telling Porter anything if he asked.

"Well, as you probably know, I had some mighty poor luck with a one Luana Beebe. I think you should let me check this one out. It's the least I could do."

Skip shrugged. "Sure. But she seems pretty steady." Then, looking off into the dripping tangle of Douglas fir and underbrush he thought to himself, "So did Brenda."

"I'll do a little snooping upstairs just the same." Port winked and drew in a lung full of fresh wet air. His mind was made up. "It'd make me feel better."

Terry picked up the tracks again on the other side of the hill. The outlaws were still meandering North. Once in a while, they would backtrack or try to go over some rock to mask their trail, but it never worked. Even when they took to the rock, a tell tale piece of loam or clay would fall from a hoof. Sometimes a horseshoe would strike and leave a scuff. Horses were just too big and clumsy to move without leaving some kind of sign.

Rain turned most trails into soggy mud wallows and streams swelled too much to provide much footing for the horses. Under a large canopy of broad needled grande fir, Terry got off and studied the tracks on the relatively dry stretch of trail. Porter, Skip and the mule reined up behind him.

The length of the strides were getting longer. Terry took a small tape measure out of his vest pocket and took measurements. He looked up and ran a hand across his cheek. "Well, it looks as though they've changed tactics. They're picking up their pace and making a run for it. It's hard to tell in this weather but the tracks seem to be getting fresher."

Porter stood next to him, studying the hoof prints. "Looks like that pony's carrying an awfully unbalanced load." He pointed his hat to a set of tracks.

Terry smiled. "I noticed. The tracks have a deeper depression and the gait is uneven. That's one of the things I was measuring."

Skip walked to the other two men and left Jake to graze at the side of the trail. "I seem to remember Carl Meeks having some kind of injury to his left leg."

Terry stood and stretched to get the kinks out of his back. "Right. And I don't recall anything about him being much of a country boy either. He probably doesn't know much about riding. I know how to do it and I'm getting tired and sore. It's got to be pretty rough on him."

"Pretty rough on his horse too." Porter mused. "Keep pushin' 'em boys. When he goes to saddle his sore-backed horse in the morning, I wouldn't be surprised if he doesn't get tossed on his head."

"If he breaks his neck, it'll make him easier to catch," Skip said, swinging easily onto Jake's back. The big bay munched peacefully on a mouth full mountain grass, muddy roots and all. Terry took the mare by the reins and walked ahead on the trail, studying tracks as he went.

He saw Millers returning tracks before he found the place the kid made his run. Light was fading and the jumble of tracks disturbed him.

Actually finding sign was only a small part of tracking. Interpretation was a vital part, too. Tracks leading down the bank could mean one of the party was swinging around to flank them. But tracks came back to them. If an ambush was in the works, why didn't the other two just keep on riding? Judging from the tracks, it was the Conklin boy who split off. Meeks had the bad leg and Terry recognized the Miller's hoof prints from the way he kept to himself.

The pressure releases in these tracks showed Miller wheeled around in a hurry, probably mad that the kid had run off. Terry looked at the tracks for a moment more and then at the trail ahead of him where the other two tracks lead up another long hill.

"Didn't the file say Conklin was raised around here?" He said, letting his eyes slide down over the alder choked embankment after the tracks.

Skip nodded while he checked Fish's pack. "I'm sure he hunted this area when he wasn't locked up."

"Yes, I'm sure he did, and so have I." Terry's eyes narrowed and he gnawed on his upper lip in serious thought. "We've got two trails to follow. Miller and Meeks are headed for the border. If they ride hard, they can be there in a couple of days."

"You don't think Conklin will head for the border?" Skip asked.

"Eventually, but I remember a ranch about eight miles east of here and I imagine he does too. The man who owns the ranch had a couple of daughters. One's gone off and got married, but one should still be around and she fits Conklin's style."

Throughout the conversation Porter remained quiet. He sat astride his black stallion and watched. Skip took the cell phone out of his pommel bag and tried to put a call through to Forbisher to warn someone of Conklin's possible plans. He made several attempts, but got nothing.

"The rain and the mountains," he said tucking the small box back into his pouch. We might be able to make contact if we were up on a peak, but even then it's iffy."

"I doubt it," Terry said. "I never put much stock in those things."

Skip looked at Porter. "You never had to worry about your phone not working and leaving you in a bind did you?"

"No sir, can't say as I did. Did have an old cap and ball misfire once

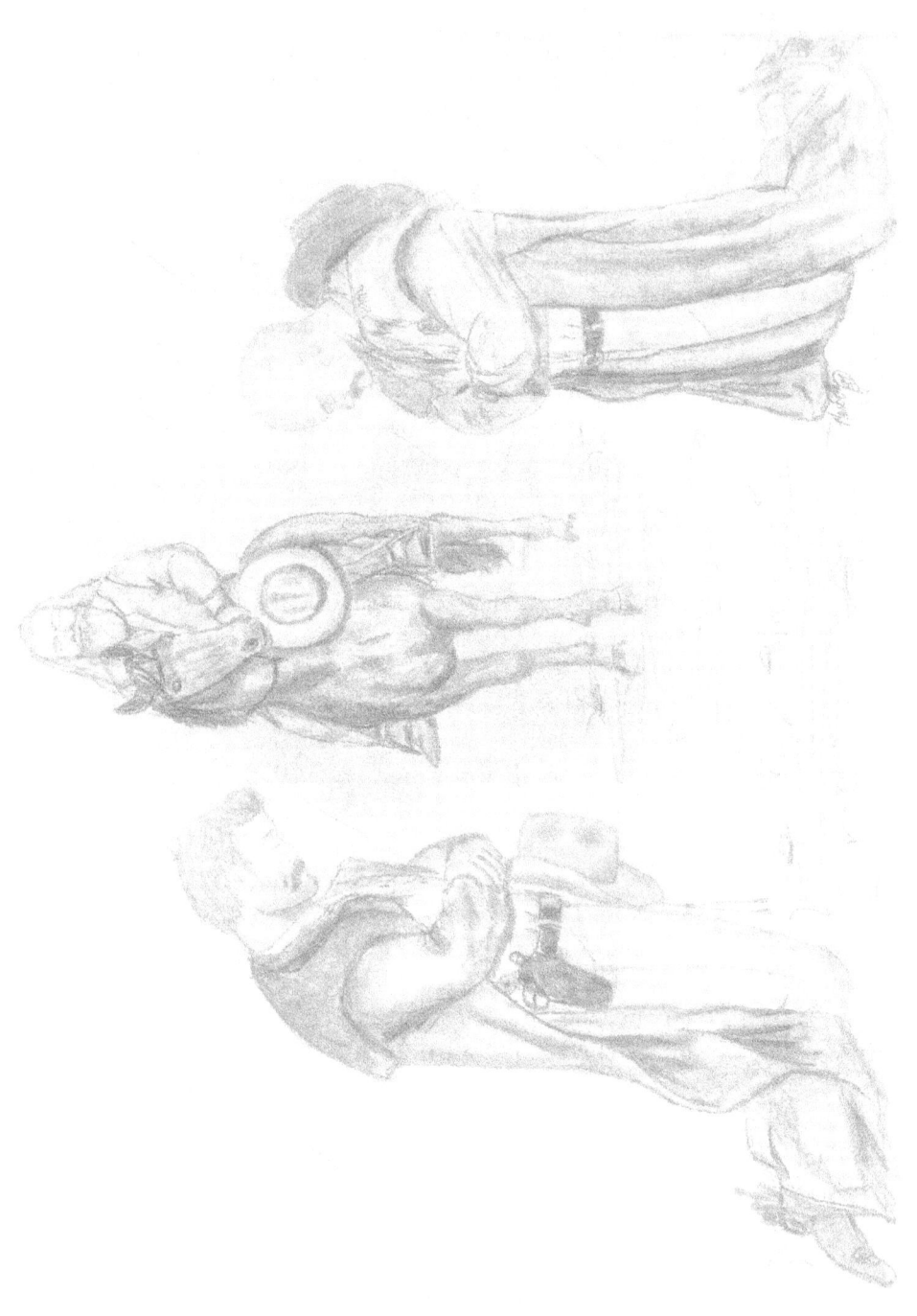

or twice because of the wet though." Porter sat lost for moment, re-membering a different time.

Terry squatted again, musing over the tracks. "We've got to decide who to go after first." He looked at Porter's passive face hoping he might get some hint.

"You think the kid will go for the ranch?" Skip said, twirling the end of his mustache.

"I'd say there is a good chance. On the other hand, he might not, and Miller and Meeks might make it to Canada."

Skip looked at Porter . "What do ya think? Shall we head north or east?"

Old Porter shook his head and combed a hand through his beard. "I'd say I'm not the one to ask." He nodded toward Terry. "He's pretty close to where he needs to be to get an answer."

Terry looked down at the tracks where he knelt. "What? Our answer is in the tracks?"

"Boys, boys," Porter said, a tired look of sadness across his face. "I am here to tell you, I was in a scrape or two during my life, and I faced a few forks in the trail."

The old man's eyes narrowed. There was no animosity in them, but they pierced nonetheless. "I can't remember many times I thought something out on my own that I didn't get into more trouble. I think the Lord has a rule: If you don't ask him which trail to take, you wind up doing a lot of backtracking.

"This is a long speech for me, boys, but since you asked, I think young Brother McGreggor there is close enough to being on his knees. You two might consult with a greater authority than I, on which path to ride."

Skip's neck burned with embarrassment and Terry felt sick. They had relied too much on their own wisdom and forgot the power of prayer.

"I guess we did sort of leave the Lord out of this one," Terry said, taking off his hat.

Skip walked over next to him and knelt beside him in the mud. The rain was gradually picking up as twilight gathered and by the time Skip finished with the prayer, his hair was soaked. Water ran in small rivulets off Terry's scalp and over his eyebrows.

"I figure we have an hour while we can still see the trail," Terry said. "If the rain doesn't get any worse."

Steam rose from the backs of the wet horses as they slid down the hill after Conklin. It felt strange to ride away from the other tracks and they spoke of splitting. Prayer had helped though, and both Terry and Skip knew that going after James Conklin was the right thing to do.

CHAPTER 12

Wally and Tracy Fuller bought their yellow frame house in the foothills outside Missoula before it was a fashionable place. The house came with two acres, it's own well, and a free view of the Bitterroot mountains. Most newer houses in the area were twice the size of their little home——none were better manicured. Tracy planted flowers every spring and refused to let Wallace even mow the lawn. She considered the house her domain, inside and out, and took great pride in its upkeep.

The street was paved now, but she had insisted on a sidewalk, curb, and gutter when it was still a dusty, gravel road in a new development. She led the campaign to get a garbage service in the subdivision, and although most of the new comers were doctors and lawyers, they deferred to her as the defacto neighborhood chairperson.

They had only been married two years when Wally accepted the transfer to Missoula and dragged her away from home and family in Helena. It wasn't really that far, and she would have followed him anywhere. They had lived in the house over eleven years. When they moved in, she was five months pregnant with their oldest boy Paul.

Ten years younger than her husband, Tracy worshiped him. She first met him through her job at the county judges office in Helena. He was wearing a pressed tan Montana Highway Patrol uniform and she thought he looked like something out of the movies. He was a big, easy going man with a loud, unrestrained laugh that showed the fillings in his back teeth. Tracy took to him instantly. When she saw him the next month at church, she felt certain he was to be her husband.

They married a year later. She was twenty-two and looked seventeen. He as thirty-two and looked forty with prematurely grey hair in a neatly cropped crewcut. He was more than a foot taller than Tracy, with large meaty hands and a round, drum of a chest. People often assumed she was his daughter, and she took to calling him Papa even before the boys were born.

When they moved into their yellow frame house, Wally scooped her up into his powerful arms, and being careful of the baby, carried her across the threshold. They spent that first night on a mattress in the middle of the bare living room floor; a sheet covered the picture window. They talked late into the night about their new house, their children, grandchildren, and growing old together.

Wally fell asleep before she did, and she snuggled in the crook of his big arm listening to him breath, smelling the comfortable smell of his skin, and feeling his baby move in her belly. She was at that moment happier than she had ever hoped.

Now he was gone?

Tracy sank back into an overstuffed couch in that same living room and stared blankly at the wall beside the fireplace. Assorted family photos hung in a diagonal line next to the mantle. There was the one they took the previous year of the whole family. They sent it out with their Christmas cards. Another showed Wally and Paul in front of the chapel on the day of Paul's baptism. It was … had been Wally's favorite picture.

Below it was a blank spot where Tracy's favorite had hung. She had set it on the coffee table shortly after the captain came. It was hard news; too hard to swallow at once. It was the kind of news she needed Wally's help with, like when she miscarried in the pregnancy between the two boys. She didn't have Wally here to help her with this, so she took down her favorite photograph, set it on the coffee table and talked to it after Christina came for the boys.

Wally was wearing a white tuxedo and she wore a taffeta wedding gown her mother had sewn. Wally's arm was lovingly around her, his wide hand covering half her shoulder. In the background, in sharp contrast to the pure white of their wedding clothes, was the Cardston Temple.

Tracy carried the photo around with her that first day. She couldn't sleep at all Saturday night and kept expecting the call to tell her there had been a wonderful mistake. Sunday she fell asleep on the couch with the light on, hand touching the photograph of her husband holding her in front of the temple.

Christina McGreggor sat next to Kate Bebee on a matching love seat across the coffee table from Tracy. Thinking it might help her understand Skip a little better, and wanting to assist the Fullers, Kate had signed up to help Christina bring food to the family.

"How are the boys?" Christina asked, rearranging the drooling baby in her lap.

Tracy ran a hand through her short dark hair and swallowed, grimacing at the action. Her throat was hoarse from crying and lack of sleep. She still wore the same faded grey sweat pants she had on when the captain came and the old t-shirt of Wally's. Her hair badly needed a wash. "They'll get by." She stared at the photo on the table. "We'll all get by. We just need time." She coughed a little to clear her aching throat and straightened the couch in an effort to compose herself. "Paul is taking it harder than Matt, but he's older and thinks about it the most." She looked up at the other two women, a drawn, used-up look in her black, swollen eyes. "I was hoping Terry and Skip could talk with them about it when they come back. I've tried, but I break down."

Tracy looked down at the photo again, her eye's sparkling in the dim orange glow of the living-room lamp. "They both know their father is gone, but I want them to understand the bigger picture. The thing is … I'm not sure I do."

Christina nodded and pulled her baby boy closer to her. "I'm sure they want to talk with them. Terry said so before they left."

"I'm keeping them out of school until after the funeral on Wednesday." Tracy said automatically.

Kate nodded. She had no children and although Skip was a boyfriend, no husband either, and she felt out of her element. At least she felt comfortable having an opinion about school.

"I used to worry about him all the time when we first married," Tracy said, without being asked. She picked up the photograph and laid it gently on her lap. "He was a big guy though, and as the years went by I saw how well he could handle himself." Tracy chuckled softly to herself. "Did I ever tell you about the time on that bus when we went to visit his folks in Fargo?"

Christina shook her head. Of course she had heard the story before, but Tracy needed to tell it again.

"There was this drunk on the bus causing problems. You know the kind, sticking his feet out in the aisle when people got on, glaring at everybody. Wally just sat still until the guy started cussing. Paul was still a baby. I guess it struck a nerve, hearing that kind of language around his wife and son, because he got red in the face and told the bus driver to pull over. He was so angry, he could only whisper. Wally never did get screaming mad. The few times I saw him angry he got very, very quiet. Anyway, we were near the back of the bus, but the driver heard him and pulled over."

Tracy's eyes gleamed in the dim light while she talked. "Wally unfolded himself out of his seat and told the drunk to get off. The guy started to cuss some more and Wally grabbed him by the scruff of the neck and hauled him kicking and screaming down the aisle with one hand. He got a standing ovation when he threw the guy off the bus. We got our trip for free." Tracy seemed lost in thought for a few moments, staring at her photograph. Then she looked up at the other women again, her eyes fast filling with tears. "Why Wally?" She said, and buried her face in her hands. Heavy tears fell on the glass frame in her lap.

Christina and Kate sat quietly on the couch. There was nothing they could say to bring Wally back. The way she clung to the photograph, it was obvious Tracy knew they would be together again someday—but someday was a long time away.

Christina played with her baby's chubby fingers and struggled hard to keep tears from coming. Her own husband was out in the rain chasing the men who killed Wally Fuller, and she was sick with worry herself. She had boys who needed a father too.

Kate leaned forward with her elbows on her knees and toyed with the hem of her dark blue skirt. She expected to feel uncomfortable around all the sadness and heartache, instead she just felt useless.

The baby began to fuss and claw at Christina's blouse.

"He looks just like Terry without a mustache," Tracy sniffled, wiping her runny nose with a tissue and trying to smile.

The mention of her husband's name pushed a button deep inside her and Christina began to cry. She struggled to regain control, to be strong for Tracy, but the fear and sadness inside her was too intense. Overwhelmed, she gave in to heavy, gasping sobs. "I'm so sorry Tracy," she said. "I'm so sorry."

The crying was infectious. Kate's chest began to feel tight and her eyes welled up. The pain she felt for Tracy mixed with the frustration she felt about her relationship with Skip and her tears fell with loud plops on the tight cotton lap of her skirt.

It was dark by the time Kate's heels clicked down the wet sidewalk in front of the Fuller house. Huge raindrops fell like crystal bullets in the bright halo of the street light and she hurried to catch Christina at the minivan. It was still warm for September in the Bitterroot, but

Christina had pulled a blanket up over her baby's curly, blond head to keep out the rain. She handed him to Kate so she could unlock the van door and slide it open. The little one squirmed in Kate's arms and nuzzled her neck with his wet mouth. He smelled like lotion and baby shampoo and Kate was comfortable holding his warm, wiggling body next to hers. He made her feel safe and secure after all the talk of death and sadness with Tracy—even in the driving rain.

Christina got the door open, took him and fastened him into his carseat. By the time they got into the van themselves, both women were wet to the skin. Kate ran a hand through her dark wet locks and dried it as best she could on the front of her skirt. Christina turned on the defrost and tossed her a towel.

"Use this. When you have throw-uppy babies you start carrying towels around all the time."

Kate took the towel and raised an eyebrow. "Throw uppy?"

"Don't worry, that one should be clean." Christina killed the dome light, flipped on the wipers against the pouring rain and pulled away from the curb. "Sorry about the cry fest back there," she said.

Kate mopped herself as dry as she could and cupped her hands in front of the vent when the air began to get warmer. "How do you do it?"

Christina knew the question was coming, but she hadn't figured out how to answer. Most times it would have been easy, but now with all that was going on, she didn't know what to say. She didn't want to submarine Skip's chances with Kate, but finally decided the plain truth would be best.

"The same as Tracy did until three days ago—I try not to worry when he's away and when he's home, I don't talk to him about it too much," she said.

Kate toweled condensation off the passenger window and stared out into the dark hills. "You don't talk to him about his job?"

"Oh no, that's not what I meant. We talk about his job all the time. It helps me understand what's going on with him. I just don't let him know how much I really worry. If I did, I think he'd quit."

"Isn't that what you want?"

Christina shook her head emphatically. "Never," she said. "If he couldn't be in the middle of the 'good fight' as he calls it, he wouldn't be the same man."

The rain was coming down in sheets, and Christina had to slow because of construction along I-90. Kate stared out the window at the yellow barricade lights pulsing in the pelting rain.

"It scares me to death to think about Skip out there tonight in this awful weather." She turned back to Christina. "Aren't you ever afraid of someone coming to your door with … 'the news'?"

Christina nodded and then grinned. "It happened to me once you know."

"Really?"

"After Skip first moved here. You know how mannerly he is. Well, Terry was out of town looking for some bad guy or guarding some uppity-up. I don't remember what, but Skip came over to get his government car for something. Anyway, I open the door and there he was with his big, tan hat in his hands and looking uncomfortable. I got so scared, I collapsed right there and fell on my butt."

Kate laughed and shook her head. "What did Skip do?"

"It took him a minute to figure out what I was thinking, but when he did, he put his hat back on and started saying 'he's okay, he's okay.' It's funny to look back on, but I was a wreck for three days. I'm lucky Terry wasn't home."

"Did Skip tell him what happened?"

"I don't believe he did. I swore him to secrecy, but who knows what they talk about in a hunting camp. If he did, Terry never mentioned it."

"I'll bet he keeps his hat on when he comes to visit now," Kate chuckled, picturing Skip in her mind.

"No, he can't bring himself to do that, but he paints on a mile wide grin when he comes to the door so I'll know everything is alright."

Christina reached across and touched Kate's arm. "Listen, I'd be lying if I said I didn't have sleepless nights. But you have to ask yourself if you love Skip for who he is. If you do, it's worth it."

"I do," said Kate, surprising herself at her lack of hesitation.

"Well my dear, this job is who he is. If he's anything like my hubby—and I know he is, he wouldn't be happy doing anything else."

"Why do you think they have to put themselves in harms way to be happy?"

Christina thought for a moment, tapping her fingers on the steering wheel. "I don't think they look at it as putting themselves in harms way. I think they see it as keeping us out of it."

"Is that it, saving the world?"

Christina smiled. "Somebody has to. I trust Terry. He's good at what he does, as is Skip. They don't take unnecessary risks, Kate." She suddenly turned back to look out the windshield. "Listen, this is bold talk for me. If I was in Tracy's shoes, I'd be a nutcase."

"They're gone a lot though aren't they?" Kate had known Skip long enough to see him off on two different three-week assignments. One to the East Coast, and one to parts unknown.

Christina nodded. "Yes, you have to learn to sleep alone two or three months out of the year, but when Terry is home, he spends all his extra time with his family."

"Or Skip, " Kate chuckled. "Do you ever get jealous of the time they spend together?"

"Not really, I consider Skip part of the family. He was pretty shaken up when Brenda left him. I became his surrogate mother."

"Do you think he still cares for her?" Kate turned to face her.

"I'm sure he does." Christina pulled the van into her driveway next to Kate's Plymouth and turned off the engine. The baby was asleep, so she leaned back in her seat and relaxed.

"That's his way, but he would never take her back. Brenda was more of a high maintenance woman. She wore a lot of makeup, needed new clothes all the time and didn't really care for animals." Leaning back in her bucket seat, Christina turned her head to Kate. "If you marry Skip, you needn't be jealous of Brenda or the time he spends with Terry. If I were you, I'd worry more about the time he spends with his horses and that dog of his."

Kate nodded. "It's a good thing I like to ride."

Christina was exhausted and the warmth of the van combined with the drone of the raindrops on the metal roof was putting her to sleep. "Look," she yawned. "I happen to know Skip would give all this up for you and just break horses for a living."

"That sounds a lot safer," Kate said.

"Or pump gas—whatever you want. He's crazy about you."
Kate was almost thirty and felt too old to blush about such things, but she did.

"I don't want him to change for me," she said. "Particularly if that's the same mistake Brenda made."

"Don't ever compare yourself to her," Christina said, looking straight at Kate framed in the glow of the porch light. "This thing you and Skip have seems good to me, but I'm not the one who counts. If you pray about it, and it feels right … don't look back. Just realize this; worthwhile things take a lot of work. It is hard to be married to someone who leads the life of a cowboy hero …" She raised her eyebrows up and down as if she knew some secret Kate could not yet understand. "But it is awfully worthwhile."

CHAPTER 13

If Jimmy's calculations were correct, the ranch was no further than four miles away. In his rush to escape, he put more miles between it and himself than he needed to, but at least he hadn't been shot. Not only was he free from prison, he was also free from Miller and freedom was something—even when he was wounded.

His head was pounding worse now, and the rain pelted down so hard, it stung through his flimsy, green poncho. The wind blew not in one direction, but back and forth in gusts and swirls, lifting the thin plastic sheet and making it impossible to stay dry. Conklin knew the country and longed for a dry place to sleep, but darkness was gathering fast and rain was falling in bucket fulls. The pain in his head was spreading down into his shoulder blades, causing his head to spin again. If he kept going there was a good chance he would ride over a cliff.

By eight PM, he had been in the saddle almost twenty-four hours and pain was washing over him in waves. Barely able to tie his horse to a scrubby fir tree, he pulled his bedroll and saddlebags from behind the saddle. He knew he should feed the animal but feared it would run off if he let it graze. He only needed it until tomorrow, anyway. When he got to the ranch he could take another horse or steal a car. He planned on spending a little time there to recuperate anyway.

The wide fronds of giant cedars hundreds of years old, formed a canopy over his head and although the rain got through, the sting was gone. He was already wet, and by leaning up against the downwind side of one of the huge trees Conklin was able to keep out of the brunt of the storm. His breath was ragged from the exertion of walking but the spongy forest floor proved comforting relief from the saddle.

Soaked to the skin, he shivered uncontrollably and wrapped himself in the two wool blankets he took from the Sloan place. He tried to eat a small can of peaches from his saddle bags. His hands shook so badly he had a difficult time opening the can, and in the end his stomach revolted and he vomited. By nine, the rain picked up again and pelted through the thick cedar canopy. Unable to eat, Conklin settled for sips of cool water. He was able to keep down six aspirin and finally passed out, in a fatigue induced sleep.

It was a fitful sleep, of one who is chased and harried. Slumped against the tall cedar tree in the pitch black with rain falling on his soggy woolen blankets, and a pine cone digging into his thigh, Jimmy dreamed he was being chased by a posse of old men with long white hair and flowing beards. Mixed with rain and grime, his face was covered with sweat; the feverish sweat of fear.

His smallish mountain horse, gaunt from the long ride with no food, stood a few feet away, still saddled in the driving rain. Its nostrils flared and the whites of its eyes rolled forward. It did not like the smell of such sweat.

Wet woods and rain precluded a fire, but Conklin's trail led the lawmen past a rocky granite overhang and it served as a perfect shelter, and kept them from having to pitch a tent. It was ten-thirty and raining hard by the time they reached the overhang. With their powerful flashlights, they could have kept tracking, but that left them open to ambush. Bright sabers of white light playing back and forth in the driving rain, made for better-than-average targets.

Porter Rockwell departed before supper. There was no puff of smoke or flash of light. He didn't even fade away. He spoke for a minute about having some things to do and promised he would look in on them soon—then he turned and left, black horse and all.

Skip and Terry didn't speak much after he left. They were too tired even to eat. Although it was protected from the wind and rain, the ground below the overhang was damp and covered with fist sized chunks of granite. Each man cleared a spot the size of his canvas bedroll, as best he could.

Terry had enough good sense left to play the flashlight around the edge of the small cave-like structure and check for any timber rattlers that might find his sleeping bag a cozy place to spend the night.

After scooping out a shallow impression in the gravel for his shoulders and hips, Skip crawled inside his bag. As soon as he lay down, his saddle weary muscles began to relax. Then he remembered Porter's advise about prayers. Groaning, he hauled himself up inside the canvas bedroll. Terry was already on his knees.

After his prayer, Skip nestled himself deeper into his blankets. As he drifted off, he worried briefly about his horses picketed out in the rain. There had been lightning earlier, but it stood to reason that if the Lord was sending Porter Rockwell to check in on them, He would probably take care of the horses as well.

CHAPTER 14

False-dawn eased across the valley just before four in the morning. Skip and Terry, wanting to get into the saddle as quickly as possible, shared a large can of pears for breakfast. Skip filled nose bags with alfalfa cubes for the three animals. Their crunching gave him a feeling of security as he rolled his bedroll and rubbed down and repacked Fish.

Terry stood at the shelter's entrance and surveyed the misty morning. The mountains and trees around them were barely visible as huge dark shadows. The rain had let up but the day didn't look any more inviting than yesterday.

Terry stretched his neck from side to side, working the kinks out. He was only thirty-four, but sleeping on rocks took a lot more out of him than it used to.

"Good news boys!" The voice came from behind them, under the ledge. "All is wheat, young Master Skip."

Skip turned from finishing his pack hitch on the mule, to see Porter Rockwell, a wide grin on his bearded face. He was chewing on a piece of ceder twig and used it to gesture at the men.

"Wheat?" Skip asked. He knew 'wheat' meant good to Porter but didn't understand what he meant by it this time.

Porter pointed the stick at him and winked a twinkling, grey eye. "Yes, wheat, my boy. I did a little checking on that girl of yours, and it seems she comes from stalwart stock. Her recommendations are quite glowing, as a matter of fact."

Terry raised an eye. "Recommendations from who." He wondered what a heavenly background investigation would turn up on him.

"Oh, a relative of hers." Porter chuckled to himself and squatted down using his cedar stick to toy with the gravel.

Terry shook his head. "I like Kate Beebe, but if I was checking somebody out I don't think I'd take the recommendation of a relative."

Porter nodded without looking up. "That's usually my feeling too. This feller is apparently a relative of Deputy Garret's as well, so I took him to be a little more credible than most."

"My relative as well …" Skip smoothed his thick mustache. "You mean Kate and I are related?"

Porter threw his twig down and rolled his eyes. "Not yet you bonehead, but the feller I spoke with wishes you'd get to work on the matter."

Terry chuckled and Skip turned pale. "You mean … my…?"

"I've already said more than I should have." Rockwell interrupted, holding his hand out in front of him. "I can't say any more than this. Kate Beebe is a fine woman. After this is over, I believe you should follow the trail you've already started."

Porter rubbed his hands together and looked back and forth at the two men. "Now," he said, as if he hadn't given Skip any thing more important to think about than which color socks to wear in his boots. "I think we have some people to save and killers to catch."

Conklin woke with a start just before five. His back felt permanently bent to the shape of the tree trunk and his neck seemed frozen at a forty-five degree angle. The pain in his head had grown over night to consume him, and the throbbing ache in his jaw seemed to go all the way to his toes. The rain had soaked him to the bone and his body shook violently in an effort to keep warm. His trembling only served to knock his broken teeth together and inflame them even more. Pulling the damp wool blanket up under his shivering chin, he looked out at the morning fog through the haze of bloodshot eyes.

During a nervous night of pacing from side to side against the tie rope, his horse had dug a deep impression in the rocky ground. "Stand still, you stupid horse," Conklin gave it a hateful glare. He felt beside him for the cold metal of the shotgun and for no particular reason, thought about shooting the animal. The haze in his brain cleared enough for him to remember the ranch though, and he set the gun back down. Thoughts of a hot bath and a warm dry bed slowly hauled him back

to reality. When he thought about the girls he believed would be at the ranch, he was able to get himself standing and moving toward the horse. Without a goal Conklin would have lain down and quit on the spot. As it was, his bad intentions and thoughts of evil things that lay ahead, pulled him through his pain and shivering.

Kicking his hungry horse in the ribs to get the cinch tighter, the pasty-faced man willed himself into the saddle, sheer malevolence keeping him upright. The exertion of climbing up almost caused him to pass out, and he sat heaving on the wet, creaking leather, trying to catch his breath.

He was about to spur the horse on when he remembered the shot gun. It still lay on the ground beside the blanket. He tried to rationalize just leaving it, telling himself if he got down he might never be able to climb back up again. In the end, through a foggy haze, he realized he might need it to get what he wanted at the ranch and slid into a heap off the horse's back.

Although it still left him panting, his muscles were waking up and remounting was easier. Turning his ride north and east, Jimmy Conklin eased the animal into a smooth walk. Vicious, evil thoughts kept him moving forward.

CHAPTER 15

Laura Lee Cole wasn't quite nineteen. Her mahogany colored eyes mirrored her father's love for livestock and glowed with the fire of her mother's Mexican heart. Long, black hair hung lose under a felt hat pulled low against the chilly morning drizzle. She sat hunched forward in the saddle, a dark oilskin slicker wrapped around her small shoulders. In the oversized raincoat, at a distance, atop the prancing grey Arabian, she could have passed for a young boy. Just over five feet tall, she wasn't much over a hundred pounds, but handled the big horse with control and finesse. This said a lot about her talent with horses, for this Arabian was a spirited three year old and had more than a jump or two left in him. The low clouds and morning rain didn't help to calm the animal, and she felt it tense under her at the snap of each twig.

Laura Lee should have been in college. She attended the University of Montana the previous spring, but with her dad sick, she felt she needed to be at home. He had broken his leg bringing in the old range bull. That was the middle of August and there was a lot of work needed doing before winter. The Cole place was small by Montana ranch standards. Much of the fall roundup could be handled by friends of the family. But Laura Lee felt obligated. Since her sister Lisa married and moved away to Denver, she was the one left to help out.

It was not all a matter of devotion though. She found herself home-sick after a few weeks away and found the boys at school too lecherous for her taste. She knew she was pretty, but the way they looked at her made her feel awkward.

Breathing in a lung full of moist air from the mountain meadow above her house, she surveyed the grazing herd of white-faced cattle. There was peace here. It was where she grew up—where she belonged.

She supposed people from New York City or Chicago would have laughed at her thinking Missoula was a big city, but the truth was, it scared her and she found a quiet solitude, she could find nowhere else, in her little mountain ranch.

The grey twitched nervously under her and pawed at the moist earth with a forehoof, begging to move forward. "Easy Gatto." Her mother named the horse El Gato when it was a foal because of it's smooth, cat like movements. Laura Lee preferred her pet name meaning 'kitten.' The rain was coming down in a drizzle and the line of trees to the girl's left was a dark wall of shadows. The forest rim was a good fifty yards away and Laura Lee was on the fastest horse of the ranch—but somehow, this morning she was unnerved by it.

The Arabian's ears pricked up and it looked deep into the black woods, studying something. "What is it big boy?" The girl whispered. "Do you see something I don't see?" The prancing animal let out a long, snorting breath and took a step back. He nickered a loud, squeal that vibrated the young girl in the saddle. She patted the horse's damp withers to calm him. Then, from the murky line of trees, she heard the shrill nicker of another horse answering.

———————

Luckily, Forest Cole was able to get in most of his timothy hay before he tangled with the range bull and ended up with a broken leg. Terry, Skip, and Porter had their horses strung out in a long dog trot as they rode past the damp fields of tan stubble running up the long valley along the Cole ranch. They came in from the Southwest, watching the treeline for any sign of their quarry. The night's heavy rain made Conklin's trail difficult to follow. Feeling certain he would head for the ranch, they had abandoned tracking and headed straight for it at the trot. They hoped to arrive before he did and head him off—if they didn't come across him along the way.

PARAISO RANCHO, Forest and Margarita Cole in ornate letters burned in wood hung from a tamarack gate to the ranch house—Paradise Ranch—and that it was. Sprawling for seven hundred acres, it's government lease-land made it much larger. The Coles were fastidious people, and the trees within the walking distance of the house were trimmed of underbrush above the height of the average man. Lush, fertile grass spread for two acres around a spotless frame house, looking more like a golf fairway than a high-country homesite.

A tall, slender man hobbled onto the covered porch that wrapped the south and west sides of the house. He wore faded jeans and a starched, white shirt with dark suspenders. Holding a smoking pipe in his left hand and the crooked end of a blackthorn walking cane in his right, he watched the riders approach. The right leg of his jeans was cut to just above the knee, allowing for the large white plaster cast that ran from the man's foot to his thigh.

Skip took off his hat and waved a greeting.

"Hello the house." he yelled while they were still a hundred yards away. He turned in the saddle and shrugged at Terry. "From the look on his face, I'd say we beat Jimmy boy here."

Port nodded, "I doubt he'd be smoking a pipe if he was a hostage." The man on the porch waved back, and the three kept riding toward the house.

"What can I do for you boys?" Cole's voice was friendly but guarded. He didn't get visitors every day, and over the years he had seen all kinds.

Skip still had his hat in his hand when they reached the front porch. Through the front window, he could see a dark skinned woman moving about in the house. She was apparently clearing away breakfast dishes. Seeing her do mundane chores allowed Skip to relax even more. Still, he dismounted on Jake's off side, keeping the horse between him and the door.

"Sir," he said, returning the wet hat to his head. "We're Deputy U.S. Marshals out of Missoula. Wonder if we might have a minute of your time?" Skip pulled his badge and I.D. from his vest pocket and held it up to Cole. Terry did the same, though his eyes continued to scan the misty forest and fields around the house.

"Marshals?" Cole ran fingers through his sandy hair. He had a mustache to rival Skips but blond and not as visible from far away.

"Yes sir." Skip took a flat plastic baggy from his saddle bags and handed it up to the man on the porch. "These are photos of three men. Watch out for them. We have reason to believe they killed a Montana Highway Patrolman and we think one of them—the younger one, is headed this way."

Just then, Mrs. Cole walked out and stood behind her husband. She held a dishcloth and wore a broad smile across a kind, but weathered face. Long black hair, still slightly damp from a morning shower, hung in shining coal-colored locks around her shoulders.

"Forest," she said drying her hands on the cloth. Her voice carried the hint of a Mexican accent "Did you offer our visitors some biscuits?"

"They're lawmen hon, and they say there is a bad man headed our direction." Forest Cole's face had grown dark.

The men tipped their hats to Margarita.

"That's right ma'am, U.S. Marshals. And thank you, but we've already eaten." Skip returned the smile.

Terry was still in the saddle and growing more restless by the minute. He strained to keep his voice matter of fact, but his instincts told him Conklin was close. "If we could just ask you folks to stay inside for a couple of hours while we take care of this."

Once she understood what was happening, Mrs. Cole gasped and her hand shot to her mouth. "Laura Lee," she said under her breath.

Skip leaned forward, afraid he had heard the woman correctly. "Pardon?"

"Our daughter is out there checking the cattle." Forest Cole said weakly, pointing to the north of his house. His knuckles had turned white on the ball end of his walking stick. It was clear to the men that he was a man of action and not used to having someone else do his job.

A pale look of terror spread across Margarita's face. "She left over two hours ago and should be back by now. We just assumed she was taking a little longer ride."

Wasting no time, Skip grabbed the saddle horn with both hands and swung back into his saddle. "She may well be, Mrs. Cole. She may well be—but we'll go check it out just the same." Terry and Porter were already riding toward the northern pastures. Skip turned back to the stricken father before spurring Jake into an lope. "You best take your wife back inside and sit this one out. When we bring your daughter back, you can tell me how you broke your leg." Skip tipped his hat at the pair and started after his companions.

When Laura Lee heard the sound of the other horse, she assumed one of the ranch horses was out and urged her grey toward the dusky woods. The rain had eased, but the rolling sky seemed darker and the wind was picking up—carrying with it the sulphur scent of lightening and rain.

At the edge of the open meadow, a small creek gurgled through a dense stand of alders, their waxy leaves shining in the dull light. The rain caused the creek to swell and jump its banks and a wide shallow lake formed around the scrubby bushes. The Arabian plodded through the water, splashing and pawing at it nervously when the girl stopped to listen for the other horse.

In some places, alder was so thick it was impossible to see through. More than once Laura Lee had surprised elk, deer, and even bear, drinking from the edge of the little creek.

She strained to hear any sign of the loose animal, but the swollen creek, pushing against alder and willow combined with the rush of damp wind coming down the valley, made it difficult to hear anything besides a hollow roar.

Sloshing up out of the water near the edge of a deep green forest of subalpine fir, Laura Lee came upon a set of fresh tracks. Dismounting, she held the reins of her fidgety horse and knelt to study them closer.

"Curiouser and curiouser," she muttered to herself, covering a track with her hand. This horse was wearing shoes. The only two shod horses on the ranch were Gatto and Sauce, a big blood bay who was half draft horse with hooves the size of dinner plates. These were certainly not his prints.

Bending over the tracks, Laura Lee failed to notice Gatto step backward, taking the slack out of the reins. At Conklin's approach, both horses squealed at each other and the Arabian jerked back, pulling Laura Lee flat onto her bottom into three inches of cold, black mud. She looked up in time to see the man leering at her from the saddle of an exhausted horse.

He was only ten feet away and the look he gave her sapped the strength from her legs. She tried to move, but the thick mud sucked her down, and she found she could do nothing but clutch her horse's reins and sit rooted to the clammy ground.

Conklin was soaking wet. Filthy hair matted to the side of his pale, swollen face. Blood-streaked eyes boiled with a rage she had never seen. His jaw and cheek were so bruised and swollen that he couldn't keep his lips together, and a thick trickle of bloody drool escaped the corner of his mouth. "What's your name?" He said through cracked lips and broken teeth.

"Debbie," she said, for no reason other than she did not want this thing to say her real name.

Conklin sneered. "Liar. I remember old man Cole having two daughters and neither one was named Debbie."

Laura Lee breathed out hard and bit her lip to keep from screaming. "Suit yourself," she shrugged. "But my name is Debbie."

Conklin thought for a minute and rubbed his eyes. Had he been well, he could have seen at once that the girl was scared and lying. Now, even simple reasoning escaped him.

"I don't care what your name is. Get to your feet." He pointed the gaping barrel of the shotgun at her head. "And take that damn coat off, it makes you look like a boy."

She complied slowly, willing strength and courage back into her wet, muddy legs. She thought about screaming but knew her parents couldn't hear her, and there was no one else around. Instead, she consoled herself with thoughts of what her father would do when he caught this puny man, broken leg or not.

She kept a tight hold on the Arabian's rein, switching hands as she slid the heavy rain coat off. She considered for moment leaping to the horses back and trying to get away, but the muzzle of the shotgun looked as big as a house and she felt sure it would be the last move she would ever make.

Watching the pitiful, little girl sent renewed strength into Jimmy Conklin's body. He always did better when he had someone to bully. Though still in considerable pain from his broken teeth, he pictured an end to his suffering, and that was enough to get him off his horse without collapsing.

"Face away from me," he snarled, pointing to a particularly large aspen tree behind her. "If you turn around, I'll kill you, and that would be such a shame."

Laura Lee felt his rancid breath on her neck when he came up behind her. The smell of his rotten teeth was nauseating and that, combined with the fear of him caused her to dry heave. "I think I'm going to be sick," she said, the burning taste of bile rising fast in her throat.

Conklin grabbed both her hands and jerked them roughly behind her, wrapping them with some hay twine he took from the Sloan place. "Go ahead and puke. I don't care what ya do. Just don't turn around 'til I tell ya." Conklin's tongue was getting thicker from talking and he found it more and more difficult to form words.

Afraid she would burst into tears if she said anything else, Laura Lee merely nodded.

Once he was satisfied the haystring was tight, Conklin stepped back and prodded her with the shot gun. "Okay, girlie." he said. "Turn around now and wait 'til I get on my horse before you get on yours."

Laura Lee felt as if the wind had been knocked out of her, and she broke down into bitter, desperate, tears. "How can I get on my horse with my hands tied behind me?" She sobbed, certain from the look in his swollen, bloody eyes he would kill her on the spot for disobedience.

Conklin tried to clear his head and gingerly rubbed his face with a grubby hand, pale even under layers of dirt. Breathing out hard in disgust, he spit and nodded, chuckling softly to himself. "Right." Then walking over to her, he took her face in his hand and squeezed hard. Laura Lee recoiled at his touch and clamped her eyes shut, squeezing tears through thick, black lashes.

"Open your eyes!" Conklin yelled, only inches from her face. Again, the putrid stench of his breath washed over her and again, she wretched.

The terror of having him so near and yelling at her, made her struggle harder to regain control and try to forget how terrible his rotting teeth stank. But she could not bear to open her eyes and look at him.

"I said open your eyes!" he screamed again, pinching her face so hard, her teeth dug sharply into the sides of her cheeks.

Slowly, she willed her eyelids apart.

"Good," said the thing in front of her, loosening his grip slightly. "Now listen to me." His bloodshot eyes narrowed, and Conklin cocked his head to one side so his right eye was only two inches from her nose. His hot, sickening breath blew softly across her trembling lips. He whispered, a sharp contrast to his shouting of moments before.

"I swear to you little girl, if you get on that horse and try to get away from me, I'll ride you down and do so many bad things to you that you could never imagine them all." He paused to let his threats sink in. "Do you understand me?"

He still had her hard by the face, and he paused again to see if she was comprehending. Laura Lee took a deep breath through her nose, trying to regain a little composure, then nodded moving his hand up and down with her head.

"I understand," she said. "I won't try to get away." And she meant it, though she was sure if a miracle didn't occur, this man was going to do terrible things, whether she tried to get away or not.

———————

Porter Rockwell pointed through the blowing fog with the ends of his reins. "Looks like he's got her, boys." The three men urged their horses into a gallop, quickly eating up the two hundred yard gap between them and the girl.

Terry looked over at Skip as they rode, stirrup to stirrup. Conklin was struggling to get on his own horse and still had not seen the interlopers.

"Her hands are tied behind her," Terry said. "And it looks like he's got her horse by the reins."

Less than a hundred yards away, Conklin saw them galloping through the mist, bearing down fast. He jerked his little mountain horse's bit so hard it squealed and wheeled to get away from the pain. Forgetting the girl, Conklin dug his heels into the ribs of his tired horse, slapping it across the shoulder with the butt of the shotgun.

Laura Lee was paralyzed with fear and saw him drop her reins to flee before she realized anyone else was coming. Gatto, frightened by Conklin's squealing horse, spun on his haunches to make a run for the safety of the barn. The onrush of new animals galloping out of the swirling fog and rain proved too much for the horse's inexperienced three year old brain. Laura Lee leaned forward to keep her balance. She tried to calm him, though she was far from calm herself.

Panic shooting down his spine, Gatto slammed on the brakes when he saw the horses thundering toward him, thick, black mud flying from their hooves with each stride. Laura Lee was again thrown forward, badly bruising her breast bone on the saddle horn. The grey stepped on one of his trailing reins, snapping the thick leather and jerking his head down in the same movement. Shying to escape the pain caused by the violent tug on the bit, the horse reared to it's hind legs and came down facing the opposite direction.

Laura Lee struggled to hang on, narrowly escaping a backwards tumble. She tried to guide the frightened horse with her knees, but she was too weak. The remaining rein caught under a front hoof and slammed the horse's head down into the mud. The rein broke free, and Gatto floundered on the sloppy ground to regain his balance. Eyes showing whites, the Arabian bolted, prodded forward by fear and panic. Laura Lee, still hunched forward over the saddlehorn, rolled her shoulders as best she could and tried to keep her seat. Tears streaming along her dirty face, she struggled to stay on top of the runaway.

Skip and Terry were riding neck and neck. Both Jake and the dun mare, nose to nose, were breathing hard—exited to be running.

"His horse is failing fast," Terry hollered, nodding toward Conklin and his tired animal. They were cutting straight across the open to an opposite line of quaking aspens.

"Listen," Skip yelled, above the thunder of hooves and wind, panting from adrenaline and his galloping mount. "Jake's the faster horse. I'll go after the girl, you take the bandit."

Terry nodded, and Skip veered away without another word, pointing Jake toward the runaway grey.

Jimmy Conklin felt as if his head were about to explode. He cursed the men chasing him and cursed his horse for being so weak. A small herd of Hereford cows and calves scattered as he made for the woods, Terry and the dun mare were rapidly closing the distance. Conklin thought about the shotgun in his hand, but he was having enough trouble just keeping his horse pointed in the right direction. His breath was coming in hard, ragged gasps and the cold air sliding across his broken teeth sent spasms of pain shooting out the top of his head.

Terry had not taken the time to draw his pistol. He had a vague plan of slamming the mare into the tired mountain horse and knocking both it and Conklin to the ground. He couldn't very well shoot the man off a fleeing horse, not as long as the shotgun hung down like it did.

Terry and the mare were off Conklin's left shoulder when he turned to look back. The lawman's hat had blown off in the chase and flew behind him like a round, black kite, hovering over his bald head by the horsehair stampede string.

"It's over, Conklin!" Terry yelled above the wind and puffing horses. "U.S. Marshal. Rein up and you won't get hurt."

"Like hell," Conklin spat back over his shoulder. The grove of aspens was getting closer. If he could get to them, he might be able to gain some ground and get lost in the trees.

Terry McGreggor was not a man to give an order twice. The two men were riding north, into the chilly, wet wind and it caught the green poncho Conklin wore, causing it to flutter and pop behind him like a camouflage flag. Leaning slightly forward, Terry reached out and grabbed a hand full of the plastic poncho. Spurring his mare up another few inches, he gathered the plastic into a large ball in his right hand. Kicking his boots forward, he leaned back hard, bracing himself and pulling the mare's reins at the same instant.

When she was four, the dun mare won a reining competition for Skip at the Ft. Worth Fat Stock Show and she had not forgotten. Setting back on her haunches, the heavy horse jammed her front feet into the sloppy mud, throwing up a spray of brown slop and bits of grass. In less than fifteen feet, she was at a complete stand still.

Holding the shotgun in his right hand and reins in is left, Conklin lifted completely out of the saddle as if he had run into a wire across the trail. A string of obscenities carried with the wind over his shoulder as he flew through the foggy air. Terry had a good grip and intended to bring Conklin to him for a quick rap on the head, but the outlaw's full weight was too much for the flimsy plastic poncho.

The young outlaw fell like a sack of wet sand to the ground, his left tennis shoe still in the stirrup. Old man Sloan's horses were almost bomb proof, but hunger and adrenaline had eaten at this one's brain. The uneven pull on the saddle and Conklin's dead weight was too much. Surging forward, the hollow eyed horse tried to run and rid itself of the man who had been his tormentor. Conklin was dragged forward, bouncing under the animal's flailing hooves across the rock strewn mud.

By the time Terry got the horse stopped, Conklin's neck twisted unnaturally to one side, and evil fire gone from his bloodshot eyes.

Skip had no idea what was going on with Terry. He didn't doubt his friend would catch up with Conklin—he just didn't have time to think over how he might go about it—Skip was looking at troubles of his own.

Catching a runaway horse can be ticklish business. If you bear down too fast, it could make matters worse. The grey had already jumped two small creeks and was heading north toward the upper pastures and stands of thick, black timber. The poor girl was being thrown around like a wet rag and Skip knew she wouldn't make it if they hit the woods.

Even if she stayed low, and avoided being scraped off by an overhang, she would surely by thrown by the cutting and jumping horse.

The runaway showed no sign of slowing his frenzied pace, and Skip, working his way in behind, was less than fifty yards away when he saw the drift fence. A long line of barbed wire, it separated the upper and lower pastures and lay directly in their path. The way the grey was running, Skip was sure it wasn't yet aware of the barrier. Whatever happened, the girl was going to hit the ground at that fence, and that gave Skip only a few seconds to get to her. Belle too, had rescue on her mind and ran on the diagonal with all her might. The horses were too fast for her stubby legs, but that didn't stop her from trying. She barked at the Arabian, well aware that the horse was her man's target.

Skip had already given Jake his head and leaned far forward over the horse's withers to give the him the balance needed for such incredible speed. The Arabian was running flat out, pushed by insane panic and hysteria, into frenzied flight. It only had to carry a girl, who weighed less than a hundred pounds.

Jake not only had to match the speed of the runaway, but beat it by enough to close the distance, all the while carrying Skip who hadn't weighed less than a hundred pounds since the fourth grade.

Never one to beat an animal, he bent low and whispered into Jake's pinned ears. He knew the horse had heart, it was just a matter of bringing it all out. Like Belle, Jake wanted desperately to please Skip.

"It's up to us, boy." Skip matched his movement perfectly with the rhythm of the surging horse, and stride by stride, Jake gained on the runaway Arabian.

Laura Lee had long since closed her eyes. She had no idea the drift fence was in front of her, and even if she had, her fear could not have grown more intense. She tried to talk Gato into stopping, but he was beyond listening. When Skip's strong arm snaked it's way around her waist, she hung onto the horse with her legs all the tighter. When Skip turned Jake away to miss the oncoming fence, she came with them, lifted completely out of the saddle. The grey, losing the burden of the wiggling girl, saw the drift fence at the last minute and sailed over the top landing without losing his stride on the other side.

At first Laura Lee thought the man with the broken teeth had grabbed her and for the first time since Gato spooked, she screamed.

Skip had to hold tightly to keep her from slipping from his arm. She was muddy and soaking wet, and he found there was nothing to hang on to. She seemed so tiny, and he had to squeeze her so hard, he thought he might break several of her ribs just trying to save her life. She wasn't heavy, but bringing a horse to a stop with an arm full of wriggling, muddy girl is tricky business.

"Hold still Miss." Skip's voice was firmer than it needed to be, and he was immediately sorry. "It's all right now. I'm only trying to help you," he said in a gentler tone. "Hold still and I'll let you down."

Laura Lee stopped screaming and opened her eyes, looking up at the man who carried her like a sack of potatoes. When she saw his thick brown mustache, like her father's, instead of broken teeth, waves of relief flooded her body. Her eyes rolled back in her head, and she went limp in Skip's arms.

Jake breathed heavily through flared nostrils and pawed at the ground. Skip stepped down and set the girl gently onto the least muddy spot he could find.

"She alright?" Porter was sitting atop his black.

Skip cut the girl's hands free with his pocket knife and covered her gently with his slicker. "I think she just fainted. Where's Terry?"

Rockwell snorted. "All's wheat with young brother McGreggor, but I'm afraid the Conklin boy's rescue was not as successful as the young lady's here."

Skip, kneeling beside the stricken girl looked up at the old man. "But Terry got him?"

"What's left of him. It seems he went back to his maker spewing filthy words." Porter looked genuinely sorry for the dead outlaw. "I'd sure hate to be him right about now. With those words the last earthly things on his mind." The grey haired gunfighter shook his head and shivered in the saddle.

"You alright Skipper?" Terry trotted up on the dun mare, a muddy, black shotgun across the pommel of his saddle.

"Fine. All I had to do was save the girl—you got the hard job." Skip walked over and tapped the shotgun reverently on its wooden stock. "Wally's gun?"

"So it is." Terry nodded. "But you'll be happy to know Wally got something of Conklin's as well."

Skip smiled; a tired smile, but the first real one in two days. "Teeth?"

Terry grinned wide, showing his own pearly whites. "Yeah, buddy, teeth."

CHAPTER 16

When Forest Cole saw the marshals ride up with his daughter, he felt so weak in the knees his one good leg wasn't enough to keep him standing. He teetered for a moment, pounding his walking stick against the wooden porch to get Margarita's attention, and then fell back into his rocking chair.

Mrs. Cole ran into the yard to meet the men and gently took Laura Lee from Skip. Tears streamed down her cheeks, and her eyes glistened with unspoken gratitude to the mounted deputies. Laura Lee had regained consciousness shortly after the rescue. She was badly shaken and clung tightly to Skip, refusing to let him get more than two feet away from her until her mother took her hand. The ordeal took an enormous toll on her physically as well as emotionally. Her raincoat was somewhere back by the swollen creek, and she was soaked to the skin. Covered in mud and bits of grass, her hair hung in dark, matted locks against her wet shoulders. An ugly purple-blue spot was already forming above the top button of her blouse and it was obvious her chest was going to be badly bruised. Her cheeks were red where Conklin grabbed her, and a thin trickle of blood oozed from a cut on her left wrist. Skip had bound the wound snugly with his spare bandanna.

"I'm Okay. Mama," she said. "Good thing for me these guys showed up." Laura Lee tried to keep a game face, but her lips quivered as she spoke, and her breath was ragged.

"Lucky for us all, Honey." Forest Cole's voice boomed from the porch, the frustration of not being there for his daughter, cracking sharp in his words. "You gentlemen are welcome for a good breakfast before you move on."

Margarita nodded emphatically, her jet black hair blowing in the damp breeze as she patted her daughter's arm. "Of course. Let me fix you a hot meal. It is the least we can do."

Terry and Skip both shook their heads. "Nothing we'd like more Mrs. Cole, but we've lost a lot of time already. There are still two more men like this one out there." Terry gestured to the body draped over Fish's back. "You could do us a favor though. I need you to get a message down to our office in Missoula. They'll send someone up to get the body."

Terry scribbled a note and attached his business card to it. Handing it to Cole, he shook the man's hand. "Thank you Mr. Cole. We appreciate this."

Cole scoffed. "Hogwash. We should be thanking you. If you told me I needed to take a message to the moon for you right now, I'd load some extra gas cans so my old Dodge could make the trip."

Cole squeezed Terry's hand harder and a tear welled up in his eye. "I … we are truly grateful to you both. I don't know what we'd have done."

Terry smiled and withdrew his hand. "You'd have gotten by Mr. Cole. You have a brave girl there. Things have a way of turning out for the best."

Skip put Conklin's body, still wrapped in the extra tarp on a long work table next to the barn and was back in the saddle. He and Terry were both anxious to get underway, but the doleful looks Laura Lee was giving him made Skip especially uneasy.

Terry finished giving Mr. Cole instructions and climbed aboard the dun mare. Margarita offered cups of hot coffee but when they were refused, brought two tall styrofoam cups of steaming vegetable elk soup. Laura Lee, still muddy, wrapped in a maroon wool Afghan, stood next to Skip's leg, unwilling to let him ride away.

"We'll check back in on you in a few days," Skip smiled. "And let you know how things turned out."

Laura Lee smiled and touched the hair on the back of his rough, dirty hand. "I hope you will be careful Mr. Garret," she stammered slightly to keep from crying.

After many hours in the saddle, when he wasn't actually riding, Skip had a habit of letting his feet dangle out of the stirrups. He found it easier on his knees. Laura Lee, seeing the empty stirrup forgot about her injuries and speared it with a small, bare foot. Before Skip knew what was happening, she grabbed the saddle strings and hauled herself up beside him. She wasn't very tall and standing in the stirrups put her face to face with Skip as he sat stupefied in his saddle. Shock having whisked away any normal inhibitions, she knocked his hat back with her free hand and kissed him hard on the mouth.

"Thank you for what you did for me, Marshal Garret," she panted, only inches from his face, then slid slowly and deliberately to the ground.

Skip blushed and fixed his hat back on his head. His mouth had gone dry and "Welcome ma'am," was all he could say.

Goodbyes said and cups of hot, rich soup in their hands, Skip and Terry trotted back toward the mountains. Porter, who stayed clear when anyone besides the two deputies were around, met them at the front gate.

"What was that all about?" He grinned, combing a hand through his beard and giving Terry a wink.

"It wasn't my fault," Skip frowned. His neck and face were blushing red.

"No, it wasn't," Terry nodded. "But I guess it'll teach you to keep your feet in the stirrups in the future.

CHAPTER 17

A cougar killed Carl Meeks' cross-eyed palomino early the same morning Jimmy Conklin met his fate at Paradise Ranch. It was a mercifully quick end for the poor animal who was sore-backed from Carl's unbalanced riding. It couldn't have made it much further .

Both horses had been tied only a few feet apart in a copse of trees about fifty yards from the outlaw camp. Miller reasoned that if anyone caught up with them, they would likely come upon the horses first, and it might give him time to slip away into the forest undetected . Although Miller was a more capable rider, his horse too was nearing exhaustion. Both animals fidgeted after they were tied, expecting to be fed something for their hours of labor. They were too exhausted to complain much, and when no feed was put before them, they resigned themselves to a cold hungry night and stood in a comatose state.

Neither horse was in a position to sound much of an alarm when the lion attacked. All the mountain miles and constant pressure to keep moving without rest or food had taken a heavy toll, and both horses were gaunt and hollow eyed. Each breathed in slow, irregular breaths, shivering and rain soaked.

The smell of the bone weary, exhausted animals carried through the dark forest on the wet mountain wind like bait. The big cat happened to be hunting in the area and like a shark homing in on a struggling, bleeding fish, circled slowly, scenting the air with her cool pink nose. Muscles bunching under a damp tan coat, she moved to within a few feet of the tethered horses. She was down wind, and they saw her before they had a chance to catch her scent.

Crouching low, she froze before the horses could make out what she was, the only sign of life, an intense fire in her green eyes and the flicking black tip of her rope-like tail. Then explosively, without a hint of warning, the huge cat rushed at the nearest horse. She moved with the fluid grace of a trickling brook and the savage power of a flash flood. Within seconds, the yellow horse lay on the ground, its tie rope snapped like baling twine and its neck crushed by powerful jaws and dagger-like teeth. The palomino was a large animal, but in its exhausted condition, proved no match for the eight-foot cat.

The lanky roan gave a terrified squeal as the lion pulled the palomino down and with a thrashing heave, pulled his head out of the nylon halter. The sudden freedom threw the animal off balance, and it flipped over backward, screaming as it fell. Floundering in the mud, the horse struggled to its feet, the smell of cougar and the blood of the palomino filling it's flared nostrils.

Weary and weak as it was, the roan would have been another easy target for the big cat. She was only interested in the kill already on the ground and when the horse galloped pell-mell through the dense, dripping undergrowth, she didn't pursue it.

It was just after five AM, but the morning

was dark with rain and overcast skies. The two outlaws had camped under a thick stand of grande fir which slowed down the rain but kept little off them. Miller meant to get up earlier, but the last few days had exhausted him almost as much as his horse.

When he heard the palomino squeal, he sat bolt upright. His first thought was that they had been found and were surrounded—then he heard the blood chilling yowl of the cougar. In the dark of morning he could just make out movement of a huge shape moving among the trees. The hoof beats of one of the horses running away were unmistakable on the wet rocky ground, and the sound reverberated as though the mountain was hollow.

Carl stuck his head out from under his blanket and poncho. "What in the …"

"Shhh!" spat Miller, grabbing the pistol. "It sounds like a mountain lion. You stay here."

"Love to," said Carl, pulling the Mini 14 close to his chest. Among his other characteristics, he had no stomach for hunting cougar in the dark.

Miller didn't want to risk a shot if he could help it, but if he had to shoot, he wanted to use the pistol. The report would be loud but not so much as the rifle and unless someone was in the next canyon, they probably couldn't hear it.

Creeping closer to where he tied the horses, he found himself wishing he had brought a flashlight. He wasn't actually afraid—that wasn't in his nature. He'd lived way beyond fear. But he knew the cat could see better in the dark than he could. With no moon or stars, the world around him was a series of globs and shapes in shades of black and grey. Most of the globs were rocks or trees, but one was the body of a dead horse … and one moved.

The cougar wasn't about to give up her prize without a fight. She'd been through run-ins with humans before, but there had never been anything at stake. Now, with a food supply that would last days if a bear didn't steal it, she wouldn't simply disappear into the woods as she usually did. Her kittens were weaned, but they needed meat to help them get ready for winter and that was surely worth a fight. Crouching in front of the dead horse, she bared her fangs, a low rumbling yowl coming from deep within her throat.

Miller was close enough to make out the shape of the dead horse beneath the tree and the cougar guarding it. When he realized the horse was dead, he knew the cat would never leave it. At her first warning scream he saw her ivory fangs, still bloody from the kill, visible in the dark.

There was too little light to aim but Miller was less than ten yards away. The first shot hit her high on the shoulder blade, causing her to turn and bite at where the bullet impacted. Shooting three more times without thinking, Miller braced himself for a charge that never came. All four bullets from Wally's forty-five hit the cat soundly and she died, turned back on herself beside the dead palomino.

Miller walked over and kicked the body with his toe, ready to shoot again if it twitched. Looking at the huge, lifeless forms of the two animals, he spat on the ground in disgust. Then, without wasting another thought on the matter, he turned and walked back to where Carl still huddled with the rifle under his covers.

"Let's go."

"I heard you shoot. Are the horses okay?" Carl stared into the dark canopy of trees above his head.

Miller was already busy rolling up his soggy blankets. "It was a cougar. Your horse's dead and mine's run off."

Meeks flopped back down in despair and clenched his eyes shut. "Dead? Run off?" His throaty voice cracked with hopelessness. "What are we gonna do with out horses?" His leg ached from the riding but walking in these mountains seemed unthinkable.

"Get caught if you don't do like I tell you. Now shut up and get going. We don't know who heard those shots."

Since the horses were either dead or gone, it didn't take long to pack. They hid the extra food and saddles under a pile of dead fall and Pete cut some low branches off a thick cedar tree to cover the dead horse and cougar as best he could. He didn't want to spend any more time than necessary, and did only a cursory job. He was pretty sure the coyotes would be on the carcass as soon as they realized the cougar was no longer a threat.

Pete topped off the magazine to his pistol with loose rounds from the dead trooper's gunbelt and looked over at fat, pathetic Carl sitting on a thick pine blowdown, a dejected look on his face. Miller knew the cougar coming along was not the other man's fault. There was just no one else around to blame, and something as bad as this could not be dismissed without someone paying a price.

Rain and sweat shellacked Carl's thinning black hair to his grimy forehead. His eyes were puffy and mattered from lack of sleep. He seemed a man set on neutral; content to coast along behind without making any decisions, and this in particular disgusted Miller. He hated people to buck his authority—and punished those who did with swift retribution—but he wished Carl had some backbone.

Shouldering his bedroll, Miller started up the game trail out of camp. He didn't say a word. He didn't have to. Carl had nowhere else to go except after him. With a mighty groan, the half crippled outlaw got up and took up the trail. He winced at every step from the sharp pain of moving his left leg. It hurt to simply drag it forward, and putting it down caused his face to contort in agony. He couldn't help but moan. Miller was several yards ahead, but he heard the moaning and turned around, staring hard. Shaking his head slowly back and forth, he never let his hateful gaze shift from Meeks, who had stopped in the trail, panting heavily from the exertion of his first few steps. His dark eyes widened with terror, like a deer caught in the high beams of an oncoming truck.

Miller was seething and the muscles along his jawline bunched and twitched. He stood still for a full minute, his horrible eyes never wavering. Then, without a word he turned back north and started to walk. Behind him, Carl Meeks feared for his life. He had seen the look before in prison and none of the men who received it had survived.

Tad Robinson turned twelve years old on September second. This was his first year to hunt and he had been fortunate enough to draw an early mule deer permit with his father. To escape the pressure of other hunters, they camped more than three miles in, behind a locked forest service gate. With horses to pack their camp, they lived in relative comfort and despite the wet weather, the boy was optimistic about the adventure.

Tad's father, John, chose a likely ambush spot that had provided several deer for the Robinson family in the past—so many in fact that the tree was called the 'Buck Pine' by John's grandfather. Taking cover in the thick underbrush at the edge of a clear cut, they hoped to catch a buck when it came out in the early morning to feed. It was still too dark to hunt, but they wanted to be out when the deer began to move. What little breeze there was blew in their faces, and the rain promised to keep the animals on the move. With cooler weather at higher elevations, John felt certain Buck Pine would provide his eldest son the chance to take his first deer.

So far they hadn't seen anything. The previous days were shut outs, but that didn't shake Tad's spirits. Every evening he would turn to his father and say, "We'll get one tomorrow Dad, I just know it."

John would smile, "The hunting's been great son. Getting a deer isn't all this is about, you know."

Tad was home-schooled, so they were prepared to stay out all week if necessary. The elder Robinson considered the hunt part of his son's education and apart from the disappointment the boy would feel, didn't particularly care if they filled their tags. The whole point of this trip was to spend time together. Even though Tad didn't go away to school every day, the sawmill put plenty of demands on John's time and the two rarely got to spend any time together—not decent, talking time anyway.

John was proud of his son. He was built more like his mother's side of the family and not very big for a twelve year old. He was clever though, and to John, that amounted to a lot more than size. The more time they spent together, the more he learned about his boy, and the more disgusted he got with himself for not getting to know him sooner. Julie had him at home every day. She was lucky.

She probably already knew their son had a girlfriend named Shelly with curly black hair, and that his life's ambition was to play the trumpet like Herb Alpert. John wouldn't have guessed his son had ever even heard of Herb Alpert.

He intended to make the most of this trip and not let it be the last. No regrets, he thought to himself as he looked across the trail. He didn't want to be the kind of father who looked back and wondered when his son turned into a man. He had a sneaking suspicion that time was close for Tad, and he wanted to be around when it happened.

The boy looked bigger than he actually was in his rain gear and orange hunter vest. He sat with a rifle across his lap and a beaming smile on his face. When he caught his father looking at him, he gave the thumbs up signal. A little rain wasn't going to wreck his trip. He was up in the mountains with his dad. No one was there to bother them and no job to take him away. Everything was perfect. The morning was cool and there was little sound except for the light, rainy breeze ghosting through the evergreens.

Both father and son's hearts jumped with a start when they heard the distant shots. First one; reverberating across the lush wet valley like the sound of a far away jet, then three more, close on the heels of the first. They didn't sound more than few miles away.

Tad raised his eyebrows up and down like Groucho Marx. "Other hunters? Maybe they'll chase something our way."

John Robinson shrugged. "Could be. Keep your eyes peeled son."

"Did you tie the horses good, Dad?" The boy's voice was a soft whisper.

"They'll be fine, buddy. You just watch the clearing."

CHAPTER 18

Margarita Cole knew how to make soup. It was a rich meat and vegetable affair made with home grown potatoes, peas, carrots and huge chunks of elk. Long, chilly hours horseback slogging through the rain made it taste even better. The hot broth warmed the lawmen's bellies and the meat and potatoes gave their residual adrenaline something to work on.

They had a right to feel good about the morning's work, but the excitement wore off as they rode in silence up the muddy path. The only way back to the original trail—and the two remaining outlaws—was to retrace their original tracks. At first, they talked of striking out cross country in an attempt to cut the killer's trail closer to where they actually were, but a survey of the mountains to the northwest quickly changed their minds. Although most of the range was obscured by low hanging rain clouds, the visible mountains were a jumbled pile of rock, swift streams, and deadfall timber.

Even careful study of the topographical maps Terry kept folded flat in a gallon Ziplock, didn't show which way might be open for travel. With the recent storm, mountain streams would be rushing torrents and trails might be blocked with tangled, wind blown trees. Topographic maps were helpful, but they didn't always tell if the terrain was passable for a horse.

Rain dripped from the brim of Skip's hat, which was dark brown from all the water it had absorbed. He sat hunched forward in the saddle, his oilskin pulled up around his neck, warming his bare hands on Jake's steaming withers—not because he was necessarily cold, but because it made him feel more secure. The comforting heat of the animal, and the smooth glide of its shoulder blades was hypnotic and made Skip's melancholy easier to handle.

Terry's mood was as black as the sky. Not because of what happened earlier with Conklin, but because the other two were getting away. The fact that Conklin happened to be missing some teeth helped considerably, but Terry was certain that Conklin couldn't have taken Wally by himself. He knew they were all involved, not only in the escape, but in the actual killing of his friend. It burned at his insides when he thought he might not be the one to bring all three outlaws to justice.

They rode for several minutes, the monotonous drip of the rain broken only by the labored breathing of horses and the creak of wet leather. Skip fidgeted with the long leather tie strings on the front of his saddle. Jake seemed content to follow his own backward tracks and Skip gave him his head.

Terry stared silently ahead into the swirling white mist, resting his empty soup mug on top of his saddle horn. His hands were quiet, though he was churning inside.

Porter hadn't said much since they left the ranch. Now he rode with one hand hanging loosely by his side and the other quiet across his lap. His strong, compact body moved easily with the rolling gate of his horse. He was apparently unmolested by the rain. It didn't seem to get him or his horse wet. He looked at the two deputies and shook his head, a hint of sadness in his grey eyes.

"You boys are sure enough low. You'd think you already lost the fight and were headed home."

Terry came out of his stupor. "We haven't lost. I just hate the thought of giving up this much time."

Skip said nothing. He didn't feel like talking.

Porter lifted a rein and the big black stopped in mid-stride. The others followed suit and their horses, glad for the rest, began to nose at wet clumps of grass on the side of the trail. Once the mule saw they were stopping for a while, he ambled up a slippery bank to get at a tender something or other he always seemed to sniff out. His load swayed slightly as he clamored up the steep side hill, but Skip was an expert packer and it stayed well centered. Belle flopped herself down in the cool mud next to Jake and kept a watchful eye on her man. He had already run off once this morning and she didn't want that to happen again.

"What were your choices?" Porter's voice was low and steady.

"You mean this morning?" Terry let the dun mare take the reins as she bent to get another mouthful.

"Yes. Could ya 've done anything differently?"

Skip thought of raven-haired Laura Lee Cole on the runaway, galloping toward the drift fence with her hands tied behind her back. He thought of how grateful she was and the dried tears on her muddy face.

"No," he said. "We did what we had to do."

"That's right. You did, so don't be so glum." Porter stared hard at the two men, as if deciding whether or not to say something. His look was kind, but unwavering. Drawing a long deep breath into his barrel chest, he let it out with an exasperated sigh.

"Look here," he said, looking over their shoulders as if he was about to tell a great and worthwhile secret. "Do ya believe Moses parted the Red Sea?

Both men shrugged and then nodded.

"Do ya believe that the Lord raised up a fourteen year old boy to be the first prophet in the latter-days?"

"Absolutely," Terry said and Skip agreed.

Porter inched his mount a little closer to the men. "Do ya really believe you're sitting horseback, chasing outlaws through the mountains of Montana with Orrin Porter Rockwell?"

"Yes," Skip and Terry looked at each other, grinned, and answered at the same time.

"Then why the heck is it so all fired impossible for you to believe you might be able to catch a couple a outlaws just 'cause the trail looks a little bleak?"

Both men studied the muddy ground. Neither knew what to say.

"I'm asking you to show a little faith here, boys—water the proverbial mustard seed, that's all." Porter backed his horse two steps to give them some thinking room. Then he grinned. "You know I think I've given you two more advice than I ever gave my own young uns. I feel bad for you though. I'd feel sorry for anyone who had O.P. Rockwell for a spiritual advisor."

The waxy, green bitterbrush and tangles of huckleberries covering the ground beneath dripping evergreens was drenched. Wet twigs and needles that littered the forest floor—and normally signaled anyone, or anything, approaching, were moist and pliant. It was the perfect condition for an ambush—giving or receiving.

Without warning Belle jumped to her feet and let loose a long, low growl. The course black and grey hairs along her squat shoulders stood up like the mane of a lion.

Both Jake and the dun mare raised their heads and pricked their ears.

Bridles jingled against halters as they shuffled to face the dark woods. Only Porter's black and Fish, the mule, who still had his head down munching on the side hill, were unaffected.

Belle stood frozen but looked alternately at the woods and up at Skip, whining softly for a command that would release her. He held an open hand down to keep her still and shot a glance at Terry, who shrugged. Skip raised his hand and hissed at the little, blue dog. Without a backward look, she tore off toward the woods, throwing bits of mud and grass up from her small black paws.

Terry and Skip wheeled their horses in one fluid, almost choreographed move and loped up the trail in opposite directions. Terry went back the way they had come and Skip made for a lush stand of alder-brush about twenty yards down the trail. Porter turned and melted into the underbrush, his black stallion becoming one of the shadows among the evergreens.

It was impossible to tell if the interloper was friend or foe, man or beast. In a dripping forest, a brazen killer and a porcupine sounded pretty much the same. Belle had it in for porcupines. Just to be on the safe side both men drew their pistols.

Terry dismounted and threw the mares lead over a gnarled cedar branch and hid in the shadow of its sprawling canopy. Knocking his black hat back so it hung behind his shoulders and double checking the magazine of his Glock, he carefully scanned the treeline where Belle disappeared.

Skip backed Jake into the dripping tangle of alder and willow next to a small gurgling creek, born of the recent rain. He was prepared to dismount if needed, but he felt more comfortable straddling his horse. He practiced shooting off Jake quite a bit, and although it wasn't particularly tactical, he could do it if pushed into a corner. The dun mare was accustomed to gunfire as well, but she was a little more temperamental about it. You could shoot off her, but like Skip's daddy always said, "You can shoot off any horse once."

The next two minutes slid by as slowly as the grey, mid-morning fog. Skip was just beginning to worry about his dog when he heard her familiar high pitched yap. There were no shots or growls, but whatever she had, it was big. That was the thing about blue heelers; they had heart. If you sent them after the meanest bull on the range, they'd bring it straight back to you, and when they thought you had that one under wraps, head out to hunt up another.

Branches cracked and snapped as Belle's barking grew louder and more aggressive. Reverberating hoofbeats sounded on the forest loam. At first, it sounded like she had an elk, but the noise was too hollow—she was bringing in a horse. Skip tightened his grip on the forty-five and checked Jake's reins to keep him still. A broken alder branch the size of a thumb was poking the horse in the rear and it wanted to go forward in a bad way.

Fish raised his big, red head and blinked nonchalantly at the approaching commotion, a string of tough, wiry beargrass hung from the corner of his mouth. Without moving, the mule swelled up with one great whistling breath and brayed an explosive hee-hawing welcome that echoed throughout the canyon. That done, he dropped his head again in search of something to get the taste of beargrass out of his mouth.

Terry crouched lower under the cedar. "So much for the element of surprise," he muttered under his breath.

The barking stopped, but the rattling from the brush grew louder and a wild-eyed, roan gelding burst out of the dark line of foggy evergreens and into the clearing. Gaunt and hollow faced, the horse was lathered from a long, hard run. Flecks of frothy, white foam hung to its cheeks and underbelly and its quivering legs were caked with black mud.

Belle came bounding out of the trees, hot on the horse's heels, and clearing a large pile of deadfall with a long graceful leap. Caught between the pack-mule and the dog, the roan wheeled and arched it's neck. The heeler retreated just out of striking range and gave another high yap. Skip whistled her off, and she trotted back to him, her nose high in the air, without giving the new horse another look.

The wild-eyed roan stood still and watched the dog. It gave a loud snort and sniffed the cool air, nostrils flaring from fatigue and fear.

Skip holstered his revolver and clucked softly under his breath. Unstringing the nylon lariat that hung from his saddle, he spun it in his right hand and built himself a catch loop not quite four feet across. This horse was on the edge of shock and though a girth mark was clearly visible, Skip was certain he wouldn't be able to walk up to the gelding.

Terry saw what he was doing and stepped from his hiding place, holding his hat out to his side to keep the animal from coming his way. Giving a growling snort, the roan turned back the way he came, then slammed on the brakes. He was, for whatever reason, unwilling to go back in that direction. Eyes rolling back to show more white than brown, the horse spun on it's quivering haunches and made straight up the hill toward the mule.

Jake was too fast for the tired animal, putting Skip off the roan's left shoulder in less that five strides up the sloppy incline. The stiff lariat settled quietly and zipped into place when Skip took a dally around the saddlehorn. Once caught, the tired animal calmed as if sedated and slid down the hill behind a proud looking Jake.

Terry came up leading the mare, enjoying the chance to walk a bit and stretch his legs. He patted the roan on the shoulder and looked it up and down.

"He looks like he's been through the wringer." Porter said from behind him. "I don't think your little dog is what scared him this bad."

Terry shook his head and motioned to Skip with a gloved hand. "What do you make of this?" Sliding his hand up the geldings neck, he pointed to a large patch of pink skin behind its ears. All of the hair had been scraped off and rusty, semi-dried blood surrounded the raw and swollen area. A bloody gash ran across the bridge of the horse's nose just below his eyes. Mud and tree bark incrusted the wound.

Skip looped Jake's reins around the saddlehorn and slid to the ground. "Looks like he slipped his halter. Probably got the wound thrashing against the tree he was tied to."

Stepping up next to the gaunt, red horse, he picked up a front foot and dug into the muck of the dish shaped hoof with his fingers. The mud next to the sole was thick and sticky. Skip brought some to his nose and caught the copper scent of blood. He scraped the rest of the sole clean but could find no wound.

"Well, he's shod, I'd say he's been next to a kill recently. He's been walking through a lot a blood. Maybe he's someone's packhorse."

It appeared the animal had rolled, and its back was covered in brown clay. Terry tried to rub some of it off, and the horse sagged almost to the ground as if it were doing a pushup.

"He's got a sore back, that's for sure," Terry said.

Skip brushed the dirt away along the front left shoulder and chuckled under his breath.

"What have you got?" Terry was on the other side of the horse, and stepped around to see. What he saw made him smile and look at Porter. "You were right Porter. All is wheat."

Porter Rockwell grinned and shrugged in the saddle. "What did you find?" He asked, but he already seemed to know.

Under the mud on the roan's left shoulder in white letters three inches high were the letters TC surrounded by a circle—the brand of the Trestle Creek Ranch.

"This horse is one of Sloan's." Skip was already at his saddle bags and scribbling something on a scrap of note paper. He took an empty Ziplock out of the bag and stuffed the note inside it. After he punched a hole in the baggy with his knife, he tied it to the roan's mane.

"He'll probably head to the Cole's, they're the closest people with stock. This way they wont worry when a riderless horse comes up to their barn."

The men stepped back and Skip slapped the horse on the rump. Feeling the loop was not around his neck, it nosed away cautiously at first and then, tail flagging, broke into a trot down the trail to Paradise Ranch.

Terry climbed back on the dun mare, and for the first time since leaving the Cole's, felt happy. If the roan escaped from the outlaws, it left a trail and that trail would lead to them a lot quicker than backtracking. Besides, if their horses had escaped, the bandits would be moving slower.

Skip was thinking the same thing. "We might be able to wrap this whole thing up today if we're lucky."

"I wouldn't call it luck," Porter said looking heavenward.
"True enough," said Skip, and the two took time for a prayer of thanks before they rode into the thick timber.

The cool weather and rain kept the flies away from the carnage. Belle and the horses smelled the blood at the same time. The dun mare snorted and side stepped when they were still a hundred feet away from the kills. She packed out her share of meat and the blood didn't bother her near as much as the smell of the dead lion.

The deputies didn't even take the time to dismount when they saw the pile of brush and the bodies. Three screaming crows and a lone magpie had laid claim to the carcasses and pecked at different spots through the twigs.

"They're afoot now boys," Porter proclaimed. "You can almost smell 'em can't ya?"

Both Skip and Terry nodded. Of course it might have been the cloying stench of so much blood, or the musky scent of the cat. Whatever caused it, there was something tangible in the air—something evil.

CHAPTER 19

The little ermine was furious. Its lithe, snaky body already turning white for the winter, it stood straight upright like a skinny bowling pin, stark against the muted browns and greys of the dripping forest. Chattering noisily, it feinted in and out toward Tad Robinson's boot, chiding the boy who had dared to invade its territory.

At first, Tad was frightened by the feisty, little beast. It was small with sharp, gleaming teeth and black eyes that burned like a hot coal. Watching it bound over stumps and snags twice its size as if pulled by an invisible string, he began to see the small animal's bravado was all show. The boy found he had to concentrate to keep from laughing out loud.

Tad and his father were both so entranced by the angry weasel, they didn't hear the movement in the brush until it was almost on top of them.

The ermine, standing on the flat of a tamarack stump, squeaking like a squeeze toy gone mad, suddenly froze and stopped his scolding. Giving the misty woods behind him a quick, over the shoulder glance, he scampered down off his perch as smooth as quick silver and melted into a pile of dead timber.

Tad's blue eyes opened wide in anticipation when he heard branches cracking up the overgrown trail. The boy glanced at his father without moving his head and got a reassuring wink. The sound was coming from the same direction as the shots they heard earlier. Maybe other hunters had scared some deer his way.

He struggled to control his breathing, and his heart pounded in his ears so loudly he was sure it could be heard fifty feet away. The crunching noise grew louder and then stopped. Checking the safety on his rifle, Tad scanned the grey line of trees at the edge of the clearcut to his left. The wooden stock of the weapon felt strangely warm in his hands.

A red squirrel began to chatter high in the top of a fir tree and sent a barrage of cones thudding to the forest floor. Tad was amazed at how loud the woods could be. He was learning first hand what his father had told him. It wasn't so much the sound that scared deer away; it was the particular kind of sound. The whisper of a human voice, or the quiet rattle of a candy wrapper spoke much louder than a rock slide.

The rustling noise started again and a tawny mule deer buck stepped gingerly into the clearing, sniffing the air as it walked. It took a few

steps and stopped, listening hard with the huge ears which added the "mule" to it's name, then lowered a graceful head to nibble on a low, green shrub.

It was well into the morning, much past the time John thought they would see any deer, and the buck's imposing neck and forking antlers were plainly visible in the open grey light of the clearing. Though not a huge buck, it was still a respectable animal and Tad would be proud to take him home.

Standing broadside at less than thirty yards away, the muley presented an easy shot, but the boy was frozen in place. Unable to move his arms and bring the rifle up, he was mesmerized by the deliberate, fluid movements of the deer. He watched the buck paw at the ground and then drift toward a thick stand of hemlock along the edge of the treeline.

He began to realize the buck would get away if he didn't do something soon and he slowly brought up the rifle. Aligning the sights like his father taught him, just behind the deer's front shoulder, he let out half a breath and held it.

Tad had seen his father bring home many deer. Hardly a fall night went by since he was seven years old that he didn't dream of taking his own. He had imagined coming home the great hunter: helping to fill the family freezer and becoming the hero of his younger brothers and sister.

This was not what he envisioned. Tad pulled the trigger. The buck bolted a few steps and then went down, never to run again. John Robinson checked the animal to make sure it wasn't suffering and then cut it's throat so it could bleed out; something Tad hadn't considered doing. He then took a 35 mm camera from the pocket of his orange hunting vest and took several photos of his son beside his first deer.

The boy was smiling but solemn. The Robinsons were not exactly poor, but the meat would certainly help feed the family, and Tad was glad to help with that. Still, he couldn't help but feel a twinge of sadness for taking the life of such a beautiful animal.

When John lowered the camera Tad, was holding the buck's antlers and reverently tilting its head so he could look into the silent, brown face.

He saw his son's eyes were glistening and moist but didn't say a word. He smiled to himself, enjoying the church-like silence of the moment and sat on a stump at the edge of the clearing. Watching his boy, he remembered killing his first deer when he was only eight. He had used his grandfather's old lever action .45-.70, and he cried a little when he saw the dead deer up close. His grandfather had put a kind hand on his little shoulder.

"That gun sure packs a kick don't it Johnny," was all the wise old man had said and he left an eight year old John Robinson to sort through his own emotions. Later, on another hunt, before the old man died, he put his hand on John's shoulder again.

"When you enjoy the killing more than the hunting its time to quit," he said.

Now John watched his son and felt his own eyes begin to water.

It took longer than usual to field dress the animal. John was an expert and could have done it in half the time by himself. It was a bloody job though, and he wanted to let Tad ease into it. He had to learn sometime—and after all, this was his deer.

When they finished, each grabbed the buck by the antlers and dragged it along the trail. The horses were tied about a quarter of a mile away, and their little spike camp was a mile and a half beyond them. John picked Tad's little paint mare to pack out the buck. She was sturdier and lower to the ground, so it was easier to get the deer a- top. The paint calmed quickly around the smell of blood and made a much better pack horse than John's own lanky thoroughbred.

They tied the buck on whole after wrapping it in muslin to keep the last few flies of the season off the meat. Once they slid their rifles into leather gun boots, John untied his own horse and handed the paint's lead rope to his son. Before starting down the trail, he checked the knots on the pack horse one more time.

The path back to camp lead through a narrow canyon for a little over half a mile, and the tiny creek normally flowing through it had turned into a raging torrent. The rocky trail was still passable but the river had jumped its banks and the roar of white water and tumbling boulders didn't do much for the horses' peace of mind. John considered leading the pack horse himself, in case things got western in the narrow canyon, but looking down at his son holding the lead, he thought better of it. He grinned and put his hand on the boy's shoulder.

"Why don't you lead us back to camp. You've done some growing up today."

"Yes sir," the boy said, feeling that he truly had.

"I don't like sitting around here in the open," Miller said, scanning the woods around the deserted camp. The clouds were still low and boiling grey, but he didn't trust them to keep nosey aircraft out of the sky. Some hot headed helicopter pilot, who knew the dead trooper, was likely to lose patience with the weather and come skimming in at tree top level. There might be no such thing as old, bold pilots over the flat lands, but these mountain flyers were a breed unto themselves. Pete didn't trust them to have good sense.

It was easy enough to tell which way the occupants of the camp had gone. There had been a shot earlier from up the canyon and the tracks of their horses were plainly visible in the mud that led out of the sheltered meadow and into the narrow gorge. It struck Miller like a hard fist how easy his own tracks would be to follow. A cold, bitter a sense of urgency and dread filled him for the first time since the escape. He fought to control himself and took it out on Carl, who was on his hands and knees with his head inside the forest green dome tent.

"What are you doing?" Miller hissed, spitting on the ground.

Carl drug a foam mattress and sleeping back out into the mud and collapsed on top of them next to the remains of a fire. He looked up at the other man and rubbed his sore leg—one of his sore legs. Both hurt so badly now that he couldn't remember which one the young cop had shot all those years ago. It seemed to him he had been riding or hiking through these raw, wet mountains most of his life. He took a deep breath and tried to strike up a conversation. He didn't really have anything to say but thought it might buy him a few extra seconds of rest.

"How many do you think are camped here?" He asked, watching Miller closely to see his reaction. If he needed to get to his feet he could do it fast, sore knee or no sore knee.

Miller studied him carefully for a minute and then shook his head, deciding to let him live a while longer. "Two," he said. "Look around you, probably a father and son. There's a Hardy Boys mystery in the tent."

Carl brightened. The thought of fighting two grown men made him tired, but if one of the campers was a boy it would be easier. "They've got horses," he said, stretching back on the soft dry bag and shutting his eyes.

"I wish it was you tracking us. Of course they've got horses you idiot, what else do you think tore up all this ground." Miller was tired of fooling around. "Now get to your feet before I decide to leave you here."

Carl stood up without another word. The thought of a horse to ride made his knee hurt, but the remainder of his exhausted aching body looked forward to the rest. He knew if he slowed Miller down any more he would never make it to Canada.

Miller looked up at the sky and scanned it for the helicopters he was sure would be coming soon. Carl lifted the lid on a small red and white ice chest and pulled out two root beers. He held the cold, wet cans up proudly for Pete to see, as if finding them might save his life. The other man merely nodded when he saw them and Carl pitched him one of the cans.

"Why don't you see if you can find us something to make some sandwiches with and let's get after those horses. I don't want to stand here any longer than we have to."

Carl rummaged through the cooler and found some lunch meat and cheese. "What's the matter with these people," he muttered under his breath. "Don't they believe in mayonnaise?" He threw two thick sandwiches together, wiping his grimy hands on a filthy pant leg.

"How are we going to do it?" Carl asked. He believed they had not planned properly, and that was the reason old man Sloan got away; that and too much faith in the stupid Conklin kid.

Miller's head snapped around. "What do you mean, how? We kill them and take the horses. After that, we get to the border as quick as possible and you put us in touch with the guy you know for our new I.Ds."

Carl nodded. If it was all that easy, things would be fine. Trouble was, things were seldom so cut and dry. There was the matter of other guns for instance. There had been a shot earlier and from the things around the camp these people were hunters. Hunters had guns and generally knew the woods. It might not be as easy as Pete expected to just walk right up and kill them and steal their horses. Carl consoled himself in the thought that one was just a boy—young enough to read the Hardy Boys.

Then he remembered Smiley Calhoun, the enormous Irishman with the crooked nose back in Deer Lodge. He was as big as a house with fists like meathooks—and he liked to read the Hardy Boys. Carl shook his head in despair. That would be just his luck to try and steal the horse of a slow witted giant like Calhoun. Maybe it wasn't really a boy out there after all.

Miller drained the last of his rootbeer and pitched the empty can on the ground. Taking a huge bite of his sandwich, he started up the trail toward the canyon. "Stay sharp," he said through the mouth full of bread and cheese. The 'or I'll have to kill you' was implied. Carl followed dutifully, but the words were lost to him. The horrible picture of Smiley Calhoun fighting for his horse filled his damp, groggy mind.

CHAPTER 20

TErry cocked an ear. "That wasn't high pitched enough to be from the Mini 14," he said. A single shot echoed across the wet landscape and caused them all to stop and listen.

Porter Rockwell patted his black on the neck and turned toward the two deputies. "Only one shot," he said. "Not much of a gun fight." Skip shook his head and looked at Terry. "Doesn't the early muley hunt start this week?"

"You're right. Probably a hunter."

All the men looked at each other and thought at the same time what Skip said out loud. "If we heard it, Miller and Meeks heard it too."

"They'll be looking for horses," Terry said. "If they think they can get some from a hunter, that's where they'll be heading."

The trail became harder to follow since the outlaws lost their horses. Terry was still able to stay on it in the mud and muck, but found he had to get off his horse more often to double check the signs. Belle helped a lot when the tracks disappeared onto rock slides and talus slopes littering the mountain sides. She seemed to understand who her man was hunting and when signs became scarce, scampered back and forth over the rocks with a sense of true urgency until she picked up the trail again.

Porter was impressed with her attentiveness to Skip. "I'm going to have to look for a dog like that when I go home. She'd make a fine match for my horse."

Belle cocked her head toward the old man and smiled her wide toothy smile.

"If anything ever happened to her, I'd be pleased if you'd look her up." Skip looked down at his faithful little dog. "From the looks of her, I think she would too."

By mid-afternoon the trail grew steeper and the three found themselves moving in single file up along a narrow finger ridge that teed into a wider ridgeline near the top of a long line of peaks. Clouds hung low enough to reach out and touch, but the rain had abated and the clouds seemed thinner than before. A grey camp robber, perched quietly on the gnarled limb of a fir tree, watched the men ride by. Belle was in the lead and as she reached the top she stopped suddenly. Crouching low to the ground, whining softly, she looked back at Skip.

Terry held up his hand and slid off his horse before he reached the ridgeline. Skip and Porter did the same. The top of the narrow ridge was a jumbled mess of rock; boulders the size of a man and weather-beaten trees, twisted by fierce winds that blew across the knife of its unprotected face. The three men tied their horses and, moving slowly, worked their way to the top.

A vast, hidden valley spilled out of the canyon below and they could just make out the tiny dot of a green dome tent far off to their left. To their right, more than three hundred yards below, were two people leading horses. Terry held up the binoculars and studied the canyon floor.

"You were right Skipper. It's our muley hunters. Looks like a man and a boy, but still hard to tell from here." Terry held out the binoculars to Skip, who crawled over next to him.

"Looks like a nice buck on the back of that paint horse. I wonder where our bandits are," he said, glassing the area between the hunters and their camp.

It was almost a thousand feet to the canyon floor. Their ridge line dropped off onto a steep, boulder-strewn incline, nearly devoid of trees. It was chancy, but looked passable if taken slowly. The far side of the canyon was nothing but a sheer rock face. Rising sharply from the rushing water below, it was less than a quarter mile across from where they crouched and threw the canyon into chilly, grey shadows. Playing the binoculars up and down the thin ribbon of trail, Skip was about to give up when he spotted movement. He wiped off the lenses with his bandanna and looked again. Off to his left, between the hunters and their camp, he could make out two men. They were on foot and moving upstream—directly toward the man, boy, and horses.

Skip passed the glasses back to Terry. "I think that's them, just coming around that big outcrop." He whispered, but the roar from the raging creek below kept anyone down there from hearing him even if he'd have stood up and sung opera.

"Got 'em," said Terry. "Just below the lightning snag." He offered the binoculars to Porter who shook his head.

"I see 'em."

"I don't think they've seen each other yet." Terry studied the two men a moment longer before handing the binoculars back to Skip. "I can't tell if it's them. Those booking photos weren't the best in the world but don't you think that big guy is walking with a limp?"

Skip nodded and looked through the glasses again. "Sure enough, that would be Carl Meeks —and the one out front would be Miller."

"They can't be more than a quarter mile apart, and they're closing on each other fast," Porter said as much to himself as the others. He was lying on his belly looking over the edge and he turned toward them. "So what's your plan? I might suggest that whatever you decide, do it fast because things do not bode well for those folks with the horses if your outlaws meet up with them before you do."

"What would you have done?" Terry asked, rolling over on his back on the wet gravel.

"I would have shot 'em, but that doesn't mean that's what I would do now. Besides, it's risky at best."

"I'm not certain enough it's them to shoot from this far away," Skip said. "I'd like to be a little closer, but, I don't want 'em to get away."

"I think you know how I'd do it." Terry stared up at the rolling clouds.

Skip nodded and grinned. "The same way you like to do most things, ride in ready and react to whatever comes your way."

Terry rolled back onto his stomach and backed down the ridgeline toward the dun mare. "We don't have time to make a complicated plan. Besides, by the time we get down there things will change two or three times."

"Okay then." Skip stood up when he was a few feet back of the ridgetop and certain he wouldn't be silhouetted. "Let's do this. We'll tie Fish and you take the mare down the side hill toward that outcrop where we just saw the bandits. By the time you get there, you'll be behind 'em. I'll take Jake straight down the mountain and try to head off the hunters." Skip was already in the saddle.

"Straight down the mountain?" Terry checked the chamber in his Glock and slid it back into his holster.

"I'll have to diagonal some, but I studied my route from the top and I'm sure it'll be no more than a Saturday stroll for Jake." Skip looked at Porter. "I know you don't interfere physically, but you wanna tag along?"

"I wish I'd have known you boys in my time." He shook his head. "I think we'd have made quite a team." Swinging onto the big black, he took off his hat and motioned toward the mountain top. "I don't intend to miss out on a frolic as fine as this one."

Terry found an old game trail leading toward the outcropping and used it to work his way off the ridge. The roar of the swollen creek grew louder, the lower he went into the canyon. He stayed well above the trail and kept to the sparse clumps of trees as much as he could. Every now and then, he caught a glimpse of the walking men below him working their way along the flooded trail. The rushing water had washed away parts of their path, forcing them to pick their way along the jumbled rocks to keep from getting wetter than they already were. The big one in the back seemed to be having a particularly difficult time.

When he finally made it to the other side of the knee-like outcropping, Terry gave the mare her head and slid down loose scree of the hillside. Football sized rocks bounced down the mountain ahead of him and splashed into the raging water. He was right on top of the skittering stones and he couldn't hear them at all, so he felt certain no one else could. The mare locked her front legs straight in front of her and skidded the last ten feet to the sopping trail.

The roar in the creek bottom was deafening. The stream, swollen to twice its normal size, seemed to be funneling rainwater from the entire mountain range through the narrow gorge. Clumps of alders bobbed and bowed with the current. Normally at the water's edge, they stood ten feet away from the bank. Chunks of flotsam and other debris rolled by in the boiling brown current.

Turning the mare up stream, Terry began picking his way along the drowning path. Once in the bottom of the canyon, there was nowhere else to go but up or down the river, and Miller and Meeks' tracks were easy to find. Thinking of the man and boy heading toward them—and more importantly toward a person who killed as easily as Peter Miller—he picked up his pace. When he rounded the point at the base of the jutting outcrop, neither outlaw was in sight. There was a good two hundred yards of open trail ahead of him until the creek took another sharp bend to the right. With the loud roar of the water , Terry decided to chance moving a little faster and urged the mare into a clopping trot.

From his recollection of the trail when he looked at it from the ridgetop, he knew the two parties should be meeting just around the bend. As he neared the turn, Terry's hand instinctively dropped to his waist and felt for the comforting feel of his pistol. Bringing the mare to a halt, he slid to the water and slogged on foot up the trail for a peek. Before he reached the corner, Terry heard the awful sound he had been hoping to avoid. Even in the terrible din of the canyon, the sound of a gunshot echoing off the rock walls and mingling with the constant roar of the torrent was unmistakable.

———————

Skip and Porter were still three hundred feet above the Robinsons when Pete Miller came around the bend below them. Tad was in the lead, his head down concentrating on the trail fast becoming a riverbed. His father saw the men first and stepped out to the side, into the deeper water. They had the horses, and protocol dictated hikers on foot should give right of way. John Robinson didn't hold with that idea. He whistled above the sound of the rushing water and motioned for Tad to move out of the trail as well. The boy looked up, saw the approaching men and waved, proud that someone else was going to see his buck.

Miller waved back and shouted out a greeting no one could hear. It was as if the world was full of static interference. Peoples lips moved but no words came from their mouths. John Robinson stepped further out into the water to get around his son. He could see the limping man coming toward them had a rifle, but the older man in the lead had a pistol stuck in his waist band. Something about the way this man smiled troubled John and made him want to get between him and the boy. Patting the paint mare on the rump he reached up slowly and slid Tad's thirty-thirty out of the rifle boot. He held it down at his side and smiled back at the approaching men.

The older man in the lead called out again and gestured to the horse carrying the deer. When he was less than twenty feet away, his smile faded into an angry scowl and he yelled again, yanking the ugly black pistol from his pants. Tad's eyes widened in horror when he saw the man point the gun and fire at his father.

The hillside was incredibly steep, and Skip had to lean far back in the saddle to keep from flying headlong over Jake's ears. When he saw Miller pull the pistol, he spurred the horse harder and called out, fearing Miller would shoot the boy as well. Miller hesitated long enough for Skip to whip his forty-five from the holster and put an unaimed shot zinging off the rocks a few yards in front of the man.

The outlaw's head snapped around at the shot and he looked up hill straight at Skip, who was picking up speed as Jake plowed pell-mell down

129

the steep embankment. Firing, the outlaw jumped behind a boulder and screamed something at his partner. Skip saw the big man bring the rifle up and point it directly at him. Aiming as best he could over Jake's bouncing shoulder, Skip squeezed off a round in Meeks' direction. At

this range, from the back of a jigging horse, accuracy was impossible, but he hoped to discourage the rifleman long enough to close the gap..

The first shot from the Mini went wide and whined off a granite snag next to Skip's head, sending the smell of sulfur into the cool, moist air.

Meeks was firing faster now. Bullets whistled over Skip's shoulders and smacked the mud and rock inches behind his head. He was out in the open with no where to go but down. A shot slammed into his saddle horn, blowing it to bits and sending shards of leather and rawhide flying into Skip's eyes. Another, creased Jake's neck and sung by Skip, narrowly missing his gunbelt. The horse reared in shock and pain, squatting far back on his haunches on the gravel incline. The next two shots caught him square in the chest.

Jake was a massive horse, weighing close to twelve hundred pounds. When he went down in the loose scree of the steep mountain side, a forefoot caught and jerked up a decaying snag that lay crosswise in front of him. Skip struggled to remain in the saddle, his legs flung far out in the stirrups ahead of him, unsure whether his horse had been hit or just stumbled. When the old log tore away form the mountain side all the rocks piled up behind it since the last slide, rocks Skip and Jake were standing on, began to move.

With a sickening groan the entire mountain came alive and began to roll under the horse's feet. An enormous sink hole gaped in the ground ahead of them. His forelegs flailing, Jake dropped to his shoulders, his powerful neck folding under his body. Skip was thrown forward into a living, moving river of rock. From the corner of his eye, he saw Jake roll past him, nickering wildly, reins and saddlebags flying end over end through the air. High up the hill side, he thought he heard Belle's high pitched bark.

The dry dust once hidden under sleeping rocks now filled the moist air, creating a black cloud of greasy fog. Skip felt himself being carried across the face of the mountain, unable to tell if he was pointing up or down. Swimming in the loose, melon sized scree, Skip clawed out in front of him for any sort of hand hold. The cloud was suffocating, and he seemed to be breathing more mud than air. For an instant, his hand wrapped around the rough base of what felt like a large bush. Then, that too gave way and something very large slammed hard into the back of Skip's head with a sickening thump.

The shot from Miller's pistol hit John Robinson low on his right side. He clung convulsively to his boys rifle but when he tried to bring it up, found an excruciating pain in his arm made the movement impossible. He could hear Tad's voice, screaming above the din of the water, but his vision had narrowed and he felt as if he was looking down a thin, hollow tube at the gun in the other man's hands.

Other noises—loud noises, came from above and John had the fleeting thought that someone else was shooting at him—someone from high on the mountain. It became difficult to breath or even stand up and John collapsed to his knees with a splash, into the rushing creek. Brown, churning water piled up against his broad back and pushed relentlessly at his weakening body. Using the butt of the thirty-thirty as a crutch, he tried in vain to struggle to his feet. It was unthinkable for him to leave Tad with these men—he was just getting to know the boy.

His body refused to cooperate, and he began to lose bodily feeling in the freezing water. The thick wool clothing, so good a protector against the cold, was drawing in the bone chilling water with alarming speed and becoming terribly heavy. The waterlogged clothing and raging current worked together to pull and push him under.

He heard more shooting, and a strange rumbling sound up the ridge. Then, the gravel along the creek bottom gave way underneath him and he felt himself begin to move downstream.

Terry spent enough time in the mountains to know the sound of a rock slide when he heard one. He recognized the walloping boom from Skip's revolver and the staccato crack of the assault rifle. He couldn't be sure, but he thought he heard the high pitched squeal of a horse. Terry knew Skip was on the mountain, and the thought of a rock slide filled him with dread. He convinced himself his friend could handle whatever gunfire was thrown his way, but gunfire combined with an avalanche seemed too much for any man.

Knocking his hat back over his shoulders, Terry knelt down and peered around the grey-white granite wall that formed the bend in the canyon. His pistol was in his hand but there was nothing to shoot. He could see nothing but a cloud of black dust up the trail where the outlaws should be. A log floated toward him, bobbing up and down in the swirling eddies of boiling, brown water. Then, the log raised an arm and a pale white hand clawed at a bobbing clump of alders in midstream. Terry caught a glimpse of a muddy orange hunter's vest as the log clung momentarily to the thin alder twigs and was swept down stream again—directly toward him.

Forgetting the melee around the corner, Terry sprinted back to the mare and unfastened his rope from the saddle. The way the man bobbed up and down in the rolling waves, Terry would have given him up for dead had he not grabbed at the bushes. For all Terry knew that was his dying act, but he couldn't very well let the man float by. Half expecting to see the body of the boy come floating by next, Terry quickly uncoiled his rope and waited for the waterlogged hunter to be carried within range of his thirty foot lariat.

Skip was the roper of the duo, but he had taught Terry a thing or two, and like most things physical, he took to it with ease. Roping wasn't much different than the martial arts when he took the time to break it down. Both required relaxed concentration, timing, and a good follow through.

Just off to Terry's right, a long yellow pine uprooted by the previous night's storm, lay wedged diagonally against the bank. It's mud and rock-filled root-crown dug into the bank like an anchor, and its thick, bobbing trunk stuck halfway across the flooded creek. Hoping to snag the hunter before he was swept past the tree, Terry trotted a few paces upstream and out into the water. He kept his eye on his target and began to swing a loop methodically over his sweating bald head.

CHAPTER 21

Porter's voice was a quiet hiss in Skip's ear. "You awake Brother Garret?"

Skip was face down, lying flat on his stomach against a gnarled cedar three feet high. "I'm awake," he moaned. "Am I dead?"

Porter sat cross-legged in the rocks beside him. "Do you hurt?"

"That I do," Skip said, touching one of his many tender spots behind his left ear.

"Then you ain't dead."

Skip tried to drag himself to his feet but Porter shook his head and motioned with the flat of his hand to keep still. "They don't know where ya are, son. It's best to stay down for a minute or two. You're covered with dirt and mud in case you haven't noticed, and I'd say you make a right fine looking rock lying here next to this snag."

Skip nodded slowly and collapsed back into the mud. His whole body ached and the world around him spun from the effort of just raising his head a few inches. He remembered getting a concussion once in high school when he came off a bad bronc. Certain he had another, he wondered to himself how many blows to the head he could take before he got the blind staggers and started to slobber on himself like a milk cow.

Blinking to clear the dust and mud from his eyes, Skip realized he was lying in a perfect position to see what was going on directly below. The avalanche came down the mountain at a slant and carried him down sideways across it's face. "I'm surprised I wasn't ground into hamburger." he rasped, blowing bits of grass and twig away form his lips.

"Pretty near were. You're a hard man to hang on to in an avalanche," Porter grinned and ran a hand through his long beard.

Skip looked at the old man for a moment and smiled. "I'm grateful, but I thought you couldn't get involved." Skip moaned, spitting out a mouthful of mud and grit.

"I'm just starting to have fun down here. I'd hate to see it end so soon. Anyhow, I'd advise you to take a gander down the hill there."

Skip felt heartsick when he saw Jake limping painfully at the waters edge. Even from two hundred feet above him, Skip could see the horse's front leg was dangling loosely from the shoulder. The dust from the slide began to settle and he could make out Peter Miller standing between the two horses, holding a boy in front of him by a bright orange hunting vest. Meeks was still hunkered down behind the rock with Wally's rifle. Both men seemed to be scanning the mountain side looking for him. Miller was shouting orders but there was no way to tell what he was saying. He pointed down stream and shoved the crying boy to Meeks, who stood up and grabbed him by the scruff of the neck.

Miller looked up the mountain again. When no more shots came his way, he seemed sure enough Skip had been buried in the avalanche. He spoke with animated movements to Meeks, and when the boy began to cry harder, slapped him brutally across the face. He pointed down stream again with the pistol and then back at the horses. Skip watched as Meeks and the boy began to unload the deer from the paint mare and Miller started working his way down stream.

"He must be worried about the man who was hunting with the boy," Skip whispered. "He had a rifle in his hand before Miller shot him."

"That's what it looks like. I guess he wants to make sure he's finished. Probably thought you were with them."

Skip let his eyes drift down stream. From his high vantage point, he could see the outlaws with the boy, and a long yellow pine snag around the bend in the canyon. Standing in the swift current next to the downed tree—churning brown water up to his waist, was Terry McGreggor. He had something on the end of his rope and was slowly hauling it, hand over hand, toward the shore. Skip realized immediately it was the body of the other hunter; probably the boy's father. Shaking his head slowly, he felt the familiar bitter taste of bile in his mouth. He swore softly to himself there in the mud that these men would not leave another child fatherless.

He looked back at Meeks and the boy, and watched the buck slide unceremoniously off the paint mare. These men didn't need a hostage. Skip knew they wouldn't let the boy go once they made certain his father was dead. They couldn't afford to leave any lose ends. Miller had the pistol up and ready in his hand. He was walking toward the sharp bend

135

in the trail, and although he hadn't seen him yet, directly toward Terry.

Without thinking, Skip pushed himself to his feet and started down the mountain side toward his friend. He turned and spoke over his shoulder at Porter Rockwell. "Thank you for your help. If you could look after the boy for me I'd appreciate it."

Porter laughed and got a wild look in his grey eyes. "Nothing I'd like better. Not counting you boys, I ain't really had the chance to spook anybody since I became a spirit."

The rain had completely stopped and the rockslide left the mountain side covered in a thin patina of chalky, brown dust. Keeping one leg bent behind him and the other out straight in front for a brace, Skip ignored his aching head and skied down the incline, throwing up a plume of dust behind him as he went. Pea gravel littered the steep slope and it only took a few seconds before he was at the precipice overlooking the bend in the canyon.

Stopping short to keep loose scree from signaling his approach, Skip crept slowly to the edge and peered over. Twenty feet below him, Miller picked his way along the trail, scanning the clumps of alder and willow for signs of the wounded hunter. He walked loosely, the gun at his side. A few more steps and he'd be able to see Terry, his back to the bank.

Skip's hand reached instinctively for his revolver, but it was lost in the tumble, and he found nothing but an empty holster. Quickly, he surveyed the ground around him for a rock to drop but found nothing bigger than a fist. Below him, Miller came around the corner and raised the pistol toward Terry. Before the outlaw could bring the gun level, Skip jumped.

Keeping his body in a ball, he let out a high pitched war whoop as he hurtled to the canyon floor. Miller looked up too late to shield his face from a cold, hard boot to his jaw. Both men hit the ground with a nauseating thud. Skip had the advantage; he was already in shock and well beyond feeling any pain.

Miller pushed himself up off the muddy trail and shook his bleeding face, spitting into the dirt. A low, gurgling rage escaped his throat. The pistol was gone—in the water somewhere, but that didn't matter. No one was going to get between Peter Miller and his freedom ever again. Wiping mud and blood from the corner of his scowling mouth, Miller stood and eyed the bleeding deputy. The two men circled each other slowly.

Terry heard Skip's yell and turned to see him plummeting toward the earth. But he had his hands full. A struggling John Robinson had regained consciousness enough to grab the rope and was trying desperately to help pull himself to safety against the tugging rapids.

Rushing forward with a violent roar, Miller threw a handful of gravel and mud at Skip's face and then plowed directly into him. Skip stepped deftly to the side—a fraction of a second too late. He missed the main brunt of the charge, but caught the tip of an elbow across the bridge of his nose, bringing water to his eyes and temporarily blinding him. Swinging his right hand backward in a wide arc, he was able to land a crushing blow to the back of Miller's head as he went careening by. The outlaw went down, but rolled quickly to his feet and stood panting.

Without warning, Miller closed the gap again. Feinting with his left hand like a boxer, he let fly a devastating haymaker with his right. Skip's left eye was swollen almost shut and although he saw the blow coming, wasn't able to get out of the way. His head snapped around from the shuddering impact, but he kept his feet. The wide arc of the haymaker took Miller's right arm across his own body and left his ugly, scowling face completely exposed. Skip jabbed straight out with two rapid-fire rights, smearing Miller's nose across his face and knocking the outlaw to the ground.

Again, the man scrambled to his feet and shook off the pain. He had been in plenty of fights, and it was going to take more than a punch in the nose to bring him down. Skip struggled to control his rage and took a series of deep quick breaths, like Terry taught him to do when he needed to focus. Trading punches was taking its toll on his injured body, and he knew he couldn't keep it up for long.

He shook his head to clear his muddy vision and took the time to eye the man in front of him. So this was the one, he thought to himself. The leader of the group who murdered Wally. Fighting hand to hand was Terry's forte, but Skip was more than pleased this one fell to him. He turned his head slowly, felt his neck joints pop, and smiled a satisfied smile. Win or lose, he was where he wanted to be.

"Who are you? State police?" Miller panted above the river noise. His hands were up and he never lowered his guard.

Skip tipped his head a half an inch. "You've already met my friend Wally Fuller, I guess I should introduce myself. Name's Garret. I'm a U.S. Marshal."

Pete's head spun. They hadn't crossed any state lines, what would the feds be doing involved in this? Then it dawned on him—Fuller. Fuller was the name of the trooper they killed at the roadside park—and this guy was his friend. He shook the thoughts of the dead man from his head. It didn't matter.

"I don't intend to go back peacefully." Miller spat vehemently.

"I don't intend for you to either, but it's your choice." Skip's voice was a whisper above the roaring water.

The Japanese call it *buttsukarri*—crashing in. Terry called it a sacrifice takedown and he made Skip practice it more than any other single move. When Miller struck out with a quick right hand, Skip didn't try to block it. Instead, he rolled around the blow and rushed past it, slamming into his opponent with all two hundred and twenty pounds. Wrapping both legs around Miller's waist, he clawed savagely at the flesh over the man's kidneys, pinching at the tender skin. The intense pain caused the outlaw to flinch and rise up on his toes, throwing him further off balance. A head-butt to the face pushed him the rest of the way, and both men fell into a writhing pile on the ground.

Miller struggled, but with each movement Skip moved in tighter, like a boa constrictor working a small animal to suffocation. Completely engulfed by the much larger man, Miller had no chance. Although he continued to struggle, once Skip managed to get a forearm across the man's windpipe, his movements became more frantic, then quit altogether. He was unconscious in a matter of seconds.

When he felt Miller go limp, Skip breathed a sigh of relief and laid his head back in the mud. Their battle had taken them to the waters edge and his right leg bobbed in the current. He was underneath the other man, on the ground behind him, but he was amazed at how restful the position was. He knew the outlaw would still come to, he could feel him breathing, but it wouldn't be soon, and he wouldn't be able to see straight when he did. Still, Skip laid there, hugging the puny little man who killed his friend. Tears filled his eyes and he felt like he could relax for the first time in four days.

Taking a deep cleansing breath, he rolled Miller off him into a heap on the muddy beach. Terry stood next to a dripping man in an orange vest, helping him slosh to the shore.

"Pretty good take down," he grunted under the weight of the sagging hunter. "Did you thank him for the lesson?"

Skip snorted and dabbed at a gash above his left eye. "I'll thank him when he wakes up. You got any cuffs? Mine must have come off my belt in the rock slide."

Terry pulled a gleaming set of stainless steel handcuffs from behind his belt and pitched them to Skip, who winced when he caught them.

"Thanks," he said, rolling Miller over onto his stomach.

"Tad," the man in the orange vest moaned, sliding to the ground against the rock wall of the canyon. A tired look of desperation spread across his filthy face. "Where's my son? They had him too."

Terry looked at Skip in alarm. "Does Meeks still have the boy?"

Skip gave Terry a quick wink. "Rockwell's taking care of him." He looked to comfort the boy's father, but the exhausted man had already drifted off again.

"Do you think he'll make it?" Skip looked solemnly at Terry.

"I do if we get him off this mountain before dark. He had enough strength to climb up my lariat rope in fifty pounds of wet wool. I think the bullet missed his lung, but he's lost a lot of blood."

Just then, Tad Robinson came running around the corner. Tears streamed from his muddy face and the red print of Miller's slap showing brightly across his cheek. Seeing Miller in handcuffs, the boy recognized Terry and Skip as good guys and ran straight for his father, collapsing on the ground beside him.

Terry squatted next to him and smiled. "Your name Tad?"

The boy nodded. "Tad Robinson. This is my dad, John Robinson. Who are you guys?"

"We're U.S. Marshals and we've been tracking these men for a few days. Where's the one who had you?"

"That old man has him. He told me to come over here and find you guys." Tad looked down at his father and saw the dark patch of blood and the ragged hole in the front of his orange vest. He began to cry again. "Is he dead?"

"No he's not, but we need to get him out of here quick." Skip looked up at Terry. "I'll stay here and tend to them if you want to go scoop up Meeks. I think the cell phone may work from the ridgeline. The clouds are thinning some and if it'll work anywhere, it'll work up there. It should be in my saddle bags."

Terry nodded and stood up. "Is Jake with the other horses?"

Tad looked from his wounded father. "Is Jake the big bay horse?"

Skip took a deep breath and nodded.

"He's back by my paint mare then. There's a dog trying to tend to him, but he's bleeding and I think his leg is broke."

Skip sighed and the memory of Jake's dangling leg came flooding back to him. "If his leg's broke, he's done for," he said, climbing wearily to his feet. "I'd better go take care of him."

Terry put a hand on his friend's shoulder and gently pushed him back down. "You rest. One of us has to stay here and guard the prisoner. I'll see to your horse."

Pulling a glove back on his hand, Terry started up the trail on foot and soon disappeared around the bend. Skip dug in the dun mares saddle bags and found a small first aid kit. He bandaged Robinson's wound as best he could and the man woke up enough for his son to help him drink from Terry's canteen. They elevated his legs and tried to make him as comfortable as possible, but it was painfully obvious, even to the boy that he needed to get to a hospital soon. The shot alone was life threatening, and the frigid bath hadn't helped matters at all.

Skip was unfolding a foil emergency blanket to spread across the wounded man when he heard the single shot. He flinched when he heard it and shook his head sadly, wiping away a tear with the back of a dirty hand. He and Jake had gone many miles together, in Texas and Montana. Standing, he patted the dun mare on the rump. She was a fine horse, but she was not Jake. Terry had informally adopted her anyway, and Skip didn't really consider her his anymore. He would have to buy another horse, that went without saying, but he could never replace his old friend.

CHAPTER 22

When Meeks came stumbling around the corner, he was wild eyed and babbling like a man in the middle of a five day drunk. Terry carried Skip's saddle and led the Robinson's two horses. He'd taken the time to throw Tad's deer back across the paint and the boy smiled in thanks. Belle plodded along in the rear, sullen until she saw Skip beside the wounded hunter. Her ears perked immediately and she ran to his side, yipping happily and nosing at his hand for attention.

Miller was awake and worked himself into a sullen, hunched over sitting position. "What happened to you?" His nose was plugged from the wholloping Skip gave him, his voice full of contempt for his limping compatriot.

Meeks did not even look down. He was completely deflated and hardly seemed to know where he was. "The old cob with long hair came out of nowhere and stuck an antique gun in my face. He told me to let the boy go, so I did. The next thing I knew this marshal is slapping handcuffs on me and the old guy was gone." He stared off into the churning water, shaking and muttering to himself.

"I can't believe I escaped with such idiots," Miller said turning up his bloody nose at Meeks. "If it wasn't for you and that stupid kid I'd be halfway across Canada by now." He struggled against the handcuffs, the pitch of his gravely voice climbing in agitation and fear as he realized the gravity of his situation. "I should've shot you earlier when I had the chance."

C arl Meeks came out of his trance and looked down at his partner in crime. His filthy face was impassive and his bushy black eyebrows relaxed. "You know what?" He said, his voice growing sharper word by word. "You're absolutely right. You should've, because I'm tired of you pushing me around. You're going to get yours. I've seen to that."

Carl was rolling now and didn't intend to stop. "See that bald headed marshal over there?" He leaned down to within three feet of a fuming Miller. "I've already told him I'm willing to testify about you murdering that trooper ... and all the other stuff you made me and Jimmy do."

Miller smoldered, his eyes blazing red. Gathering himself in a savage growl, he attempted a lunge at the other man. He hadn't made it a foot before he caught the mudcaked toe of Skip's boot, hard in his ribs.

"I'd like for you to keep doing that," Skip said, standing over the gasping outlaw. Belle sensed her master's mood and bared long, ivory fangs. Exhausted and beaten, Miller relaxed.

"About Jake," Skip said, scratching the heeler behind the ears to calm her. "I'm obliged to you." Terry threw his saddle across a high, round boulder to keep it out of the water. It seemed lonely there without Jake under it.

"Welcome." Terry nodded. He walked over to his friend and put a hand on his shoulder. "He was hurt bad."

"I know ... I know," Skip said. He sank back against a cool, wet boulder along the edge of the thundering creek, hugged his dog, and felt the cool spray on his face.

Terry rode the dun mare back to the crest of the ridge and retrieved Fish who had worn a circle in the mud around the tree where he was tied. The mule's huge ears perked when he saw his mare approach and he cut loose in joyous song. The cel phone worked from the ridgeline and Terry was able to make crackling contact with the State Police dispatcher. It took only forty-five minutes to get a Sanders County unit past the locked Forest Service gate and down to the Robinson's camp. The two deputies helped carry John Robinson out of the canyon on a make shift litter and Skip rode out on the dun mare. The clouds were still thinning, but it was getting late and an air evacuation of Robinson was out of the question. It was decided without debate that he and his son should go out with the county deputies until they could rendezvous with an ambulance closer to civilization.

Terry built a small fire against the encroaching darkness and he and Skip stayed with the two prisoners until a state unit arrived a short time later.

Lieutenant Forbisher climbed out of his commandeered Forest Service Jeep and sauntered past the two marshals. His face showed the jubilant gloat of a man who's plan had worked. Walking straight to where the prisoners sat, the lieutenant prodded Miller with a spit shined boot.

"Looks like you've been working hard," Miller said, shaking his head at the spotless footwear.

Forbisher stiffened but let the remark pass. It didn't matter what men like Miller had to say. He had already alerted the media back in Missoula and envisioned his triumphant return. The lieutenant grinned to himself. This was the stuff captains were made of.

He prodded the outlaw again, a bit harder this time. "On your feet!" Miller, sick of being kicked, got to his feet with a groan.

"You too," Forbisher barked to Meeks, who sat cross legged in his irons, staring at the dancing flames of the fire.

"It all happened so fast," Meeks whined, a pitiful look in his eye. "I didn't mean for the cop to get killed, you know."

"Well, he did, and it doesn't look good for either of you. Now, get moving!"

Forbisher's arrogant attitude made Terry chuckle to himself. It never ceased to amaze him how some officers swooped out of nowhere, once dangerous killers were handcuffed, and started barking orders as if they were insolent school kids. If it would have been anybody else but Miller, Terry would have asked for his handcuffs back just to watch what happened.

Satisfied he had gotten the prisoners' attention, Forbisher passed them off to his young freckled-faced assistant and turned to the two marshals.

"The state of Montana appreciates what you did in bringing these men to justice," he said, because he thought he had to. "The sheriff is on his way up. He and his men will help you with the animals and get you back to town." With that, he walked back to his prisoners without another word and motioned for the red headed trooper to drive him off the mountain.

Terry handed Skip one of the Robinson's rootbeers and sat down on top of the red cooler. They watched the Jeep slither out of view down the deep muddy ruts of the mountain road.

Porter Rockwell's voice came from the gathering twilight behind them as he walked into the glowing ring of campfire. "Well, I must say it worked out right fine." He stood a few feet from the flames, his long locks orange in the flickering light. A mischievous grin crossed his face and he pointed at Skip with a coiled rawhide lariat. "You don't look so good. You think that Beebe gal'll still have ya?"

Skip found it hurt his ribs to chuckle. "I don't know. I hope so."

All three looked in silence at the comforting fire, content to share the time together as comrades. It was Terry who broke the silence.

"I'm still not certain why you came back." He looked down at his filthy boots and kicked at a tuft of grass. "But it's been a pleasure to meet you."

"Same here," said Skip. "I'm pretty sure you saved my life back there in the avalanche."

Porter put a finger to his lips and winked. "Let's keep that between us. Besides, you boys saved a life or two today. Did you think I was gonna let you steal all the fun? As for why I came, well … let me tell you a little story."

He hunkered down by the fire and warmed his hands, letting the coiled rope swing off his thumb. His steel grey eyes reflected the dancing flames and entranced the other two. "You both know I had my share of high adventure. All my life I just tried to do what was right. I don't have to tell you, I got a pretty sorry reputation doing it." Rockwell wagged a finger at the deputies. "These times call for hard men to do some mighty hard things, just like mine did—but you have to keep your faith." He stood and paced back and forth beside the fire. "I battled with it for a time—became an expert, you might say. I had a little help now and then myself."

"From who?" Skip asked.

"Don't matter, but I did. So, I thought I might return the favor." Porter looked behind him into the black shadow of the canyon. "I gotta git," he said twirling the catch rope in his hands.

"Now this is over, what'll you do?" Skip voiced what Terry was thinking.

Porter smiled and shook out a loop. "Oh, I don't rightly know. Just now, I think I'll saunter over and catch me a stout bay horse. That black nag of mine don't ever get tired, but I might want me a remount once in a while." He winked at Skip. "You wouldn't mind if I used him a bit would you?"

Skip felt a lump form in his throat. "I'd be more than honored." He stood and moved to take off his hat, forgetting it wasn't there.

"Well, I hear your ride coming, and I've got work to do. I may slip up to your campfire now and again … just to stretch my wings so to speak—if you don't mind."

"You know better than that," Terry said reverently.

The old gunfighter walked to the edge of camp, then turned to Skip with an afterthought. "Oh, I almost forgot," he said. "I found your hat back there in the rubble. It seemed important to you, so I put it by your saddle. No sense in losing a good horse and a good hat in the same day, eh?"

"I wish we could shake your hand before you leave." Terry smiled a thin, solemn smile.

Rockwell shook his head. "I do too boys, but you know what the Prophet Joseph said about shaking hands with heavenly beings—and you know I ain't no angel—I'm Orrin Porter Rockwell!"

With that he vanished, quietly, without fanfare, leaving them in the twilight by the flickering embers of a dying fire.

He was only gone a moment before the Sanders County Cavalry arrived in force. Both Skip's eyes were going purple and a golf ball sized goose egg had formed over his left brow. "You need a doctor son," Sheriff Nelson said, climbing out of his four-wheel drive. He played the bright beam of his flashlight across Skip's face and spit a golden slurry of tobacco juice into the mud.

"I think he might be right," Skip said, looking at Terry. "I'm seeing two of you and that's a little more than a body can handle."

Nelson opened the back door to his Suburban and gave a theatrical flourish with his hat in hand. "Your chariot awaits 'O wise and cunning bandit catchers.' My men'll take care of the horses and your mule."

"And the boy's deer?" Terry asked.

"I'll take care of that myself, while you two are getting situated. The Robinsons are good Sanders county Republicans after all."Belle jumped in first and gave Skip a chastising bark for being so slow. "She acts like she's worried about you," Terry said.

Skip clutched his ribs and moved slowly to the truck. "And well she should be."

"Quit your belly-achin'," Terry said, but he gently helped his friend into the vehicle.

CHAPTER 23
Wednesday

Brilliant sunshine contrasted sharply with the preceding dreary rain and fog. Wally Fuller was a man with many friends and the streets in front of the hillside cemetery were lined with vehicles from all over the West. It was a standing room only service at the chapel that morning. Every folding chair in the building had been pressed into service and the overflow and gymnasium were full up to the stage. Ward members, relatives, and friends of the family were nearly outnumbered by law enforcement from the Rocky Mountain region. One of their own had fallen, and they dealt with their own mortality.

Forbisher showed up dressed in a dapper grey suit—with no belt. His sprite of a wife was surprisingly sweet, and offered sincere condolences to the family. Even at the funeral, Forbisher couldn't help but dog the captain's every move with such determination, the harried man finally had to hide in the men's room just to get some peace.

Terry and Skip had a good laugh from Forbisher's rendition of the manhunt for the Missoula paper. 'Highway Patrol Lieutenant Brings Killers off Mountain' was the headline, which when you thought about it, was absolutely true.

The snaking procession from the chapel to the cemetery was a slow, almost tedious affair. An honor guard of ten polished, white Montana Highway Patrol cars led the way, blue lights flashing and sirens blaring at every intersection. Tracy and the boys followed the hearse in a long gunmetal grey limo provided by the funeral home. Behind them were friends and family, and a flashing, blinking tail of fifty more marked police vehicles from as far away as Dallas.

Skip found himself overwhelmed by the large number of people. His head pounded from the bumps he got in the rockslide, not to mention his scrap with Miller. He found it extremely difficult to get a lung full of air. The doctor told him he had escaped a concussion, but at least three ribs were broken and several more badly bruised. His vision was blurred through a swollen left eye and for this reason, among others, he had opted to ride with Kate in her little brown Plymouth.

He and Terry were both near exhaustion, but neither would hear of letting anyone else take their place as pall bearers. Bishop Morrison, seeing the large numbers of nonmembers present at the graveside dedication, took the opportunity to speak a few minutes about the plan of salvation and eternity, sneaking in a bit of missionary work on Fuller's behalf. Skip listened and smiled, thinking how much Wally would have liked the touch.

After the graveside service, everyone milled around, enjoying the warming sunshine and paying their respects to Tracy, who stood quietly by the shiny grey casket. She seemed to be dealing with everything now, though she still carried her photograph in a lace-gloved hand. Both her sons stood beside her, each feeling his own kind of loss and pain along with the pain of his mother. Both handled their hurt in different ways. Little Matt cried softly during the funeral but felt more relaxed once they got outside. Paul spent his time doting on his mother and trying to comfort her. The pressure of his father's death was tremendous, but the thought of his mother's never ending sadness dragged him down the most. Today she seemed happier, and because of that, he relaxed and dealt with his own grief.

"I know that's not him in the box," Tracy said, looking at the casket. Terry and Christina stood beside her, a tight family unit; Terry clutching his boys and Christina clutching him. "He's somewhere better now." Her voice trailed off, more in deep thought than sadness, and she turned to Christina. "Do you believe in dreams?"

Christina nodded and Terry smiled, rubbing the top of Zane's blond head. "I believe in a lot of things I wasn't sure of before," he said.

"Well, I had a wonderful one last night. Wally was there." Tracy smiled wearily and pushed her dark bangs out of her eyes. Christina wiped away a tear.

"He told me not to worry and said you and Skip would help with the boys. He said he was very busy but he missed me." She dabbed at her nose with a tissue. "Who knows how long dreams last—but this one seemed to go on all night. We sat for a long time, him holding me in his big arms. Before he left, he promised me we'd be together again … forever. Then he kissed me, the way he used to kiss me, the way he kissed me Friday night before he went to work—then he walked away."

Paul stared down at the ground and dug the toe of his black Sunday shoe into the mud. "I had the same dream almost," he said, patting his mother on the arm to comfort her. "It's like Dad was coming to say goodbye. He told me to be strong and take care of the family." Paul was a big boy, not much shorter than his mother, with a big heart like his father. He took his new responsibility seriously.

"I saw Daddy too," said little Matt, with a huge grin. "Only I wasn't sleeping. He came into the room and tucked me in last night. He told me to be happy and we'd all be together again before I knew it."

Tracy smiled and tousled her little boy's hair. "You have a wonderful Daddy," she said, allowing herself another little cry.

Kate leaned back against the car and looked softly at the milling crowd as they filed past the grave and back to their vehicles to get on with their respective lives. Skip stood next to her, his hat in his hand, saying nothing. He wore his favorite dark grey suit and most of a roll of surgical tape in one place or another.

The days of rain washed the air and it was clean and dazzling in the mid morning light. The faint scent of the herbal shampoo Kate used carried vaguely in the breeze and put Skip in a dreamy, contented mood.

Her jaw was set and she bit on her bottom lip in thought.

"So," she said, looking out across the rolling emerald field of grey and white headstones. "You could end up here just like Wally."

Skip gave nodding grunt. "Kate, this is where we all end up; some sooner, some later."

"I know," she shrugged. "I had a long talk with Christina about us while you were away. She helped me understand things better."

"I'm relieved to hear you still think there is an us to talk about."

More silence, then Skip said, "A long talk, huh? I hope she didn't tell you all my little secrets."

"What are they? I'll tell you if she did."

Skip touched the dark purple knot over his eye. "I bruise easy for one thing."

Kate stood away from her car and suddenly threw her arms around Skip's neck. Startled but happy, he let his own hands wrap around her narrow waist. He didn't even mind his hurting ribs. She looked up at him and touched the swollen edge of his strong, square jaw. Running the tip of her finger along the dark half moons under each eye and across the bridge of his nose, she looked at his wounded, wind-chapped face. "You look tough," she said, letting her finger slide down his thick mustache to his bottom lip. "I don't know how any girl could resist you."

"Well, it's been done before."

Kate nodded. "So I hear ... She didn't know what she was losing."

"And you think you do?"

"Pretty sure."

Skip took Kate by a shoulder and tilted her chin up with the tip of his finger. "I love you," he said, and after he took in the beauty of her soft, round face he pulled her back against him.

"I love you too," her voice was muffled against his chest. They stood together for a moment, enjoying the closeness before she wriggled free and looked back up at him with a raised eyebrow. "Just so you know though, I don't think you should be doing anything drastic off my back porch ... until we get a few things settled."

www.ingramcontent.com/pod-product-compliance
Lightning Source LLC
Chambersburg PA
CBHW060423260626
47161CB00005B/1760